Fates, Mates, and Apple Turnovers

A Cupid's Valentine Spin-Off

DANI GRAY
&
LISA OLIVER

Copyright © 2019

Fates, Mates and Apple Turnovers is a work of fiction. Names, characters, places and incidents are either the product of the author's imagination or are used fictitiously and any resemblance to any actual persons, living or dead, events or locales is entirely coincidental.

Table of Contents

Dedication

Firstly, I want to give a huge shout out to Lisa. When she suggested this, I almost cried at the thought of working with someone who has not only help mentor me, but has become like a family member. She has offered me so much, for which I feel I give her too little in return.

Thank you for being the amazing person you are!

Second, to my family. You put up with me always shushing you so I can type out all the crazy idea's that are in my head. Thank you for putting up with me, love you guys!

Chapter One

Peter Ames knew what he was doing was disgusting, but he was so hungry. He wasn't able to find work, no one would hire him since he didn't have an address or any documents. The last time someone beat him up, they stole his backpack with his wallet in it. He really didn't care about that, but they took the only picture he had of his mom. He still cried every time he thought about losing that picture.

Peter frowned, his fingers were shaking. Actually, it was more than his fingers, his whole body was wracked with faint tremors. Stealing his nerves, he carefully opened the lid of the dumpster, forcing himself up and over the lip of it which was almost as tall as he was. Peter loved the smells that emanated from the bakery – unfortunately, the dumpster didn't smell anything like freshly baked breads and sweet treats. But Peter had no choice. He couldn't walk through the front door – not without any money in his pocket. As the shaking in his limbs increased, he prayed he'd find something that would sit right in his gut.

So intent on moving around the dumpster, opening one foul smelling garbage bag after another, Peter didn't realize someone had come out the back door of the premises until sharp words made him freeze.

"Can I help you with something?"

Peter spun around so fast he fell over in the bags.

"Eww." Peter shook his hand trying to get the wet coffee grinds off it.

"Why are you in my garbage?" A blond, really pretty face peered over the edge of the dumpster. He didn't look angry – more curious than anything.

"Your dumpster? I'm sorry, just let me get out. I won't bother you again." Peter scrambled about, trying to gain his footing, determined not to cry at the thought of not getting anything to eat.

"I'm not stopping you getting out, but you still haven't told me why you're in my garbage?"

"Cause I'm so hungry, and your shop always smells so good," Peter said, grabbing hold of his stomach. He was on his feet, out of the dumpster, but the shakiness was still running through his limbs.

"I always give my leftovers to the shelter, why don't you go there and get something to eat?" The blond tilted his head as though it was the most obvious thing in the world for a poor person to do.

"I can't go to the shelter." Peter wrapped his arms tighter around his aching stomach.

"Why not? That's what those places are there for, to help feed and house the homeless. That's why all my leftovers go to them every day. Honestly, I can call the guy and let him know to expect you if you like?"

Peter hung his head in shame. "I can't be seen around there. It's not safe for me. There are a couple of guys there who won't leave me alone, always pushing me around and when I heard what they were going to do to me the next time they saw me, I ran and never went back. I can't fight them."

"What were they going to do." The pretty blond man asked, and he looked mad.

Peter took a step back, getting ready to run.

"They were going to rape me and leave my body in a dumpster just like this one," Peter whispered.

"What!"

Peter cringed at the volume of the blond's voice, willing his limbs to cooperate as he readied himself to run. But something was stopping him.

Looking down, he saw the man had put his hand on his arm, but wasn't trying to hold him. There was no pressure in the grip.

"Please, let me help you."

Moving so he could look into the man's eyes, Peter could see the honesty in the request.

"Why would you help someone like me? I just tried to steal from you."

The pretty blond snorted. "I don't consider it stealing when someone tries to take something I've thrown away. And as for helping you, I want to. Even though I have never been in your situation, I refuse to stand by and not help." He took his hand off Peter's arm and held out his hand to him instead.

"Hi, I'm Cupid. I own the store. Would you like to come in and get something to eat?"

Shaking Cupid's hand, Peter shook his head.

"I wish I could, but I don't have any money."

"Ah, a proud man. I like it. Would you consider an exchange, I will give you enough food to feed yourself today, and you can do my dishes in return?"

"Can I do some extra work and maybe get some food for my twin?" Peter asked, his hope rising just a little bit. "I don't mind working hard, but it's been days since we've eaten."

"Sure, I have a lot of dishes that need to be done. The last guy who worked here quit to move with his girlfriend because she had a better paying job offer."

"I'll work as much as you need me to." Peter knew he had tears in his eyes. "I'm so grateful that you are helping me like this."

"Come on," Cupid turned to walk back into the shop. "Let's get you cleaned up and fed, then you can begin the dishes."

Following Cupid, Peter timidly stepped into the bakery to the most amazing smells. When his stomach let out a loud rumble, Peter was sure his face was about to start on fire with how embarrassed he was.

Looking up when he heard laughter, he was upset at hearing Cupid laugh.

"I'm going to take that as a compliment to my food," Cupid said, smiling at him.

Peter ducked his head, even more embarrassed at thinking that Cupid was laughing at him.

"Come over here and have a seat."

Moving in the direction of where Cupid pointed, he was surprised to see a small table with two chairs.

"My husband and I will sit here and eat together when he has a chance to come by. We try to eat as many meals together as we can, but our jobs sometimes makes that difficult."

"That's so great." Peter smiled at his new friend. "I know it's hard to spend time together when you have time conflicts. My brother and I used to spend a lot of time together, but when we began to work, it became harder and now…." He trailed off. He didn't want to think about how badly their lives had changed, especially when all he could focus on was the delicious smells of fresh baked goods.

Cupid came back over to the table with a couple of plates in his hands. Passing one of the plates to him, Peter was so excited at the amount of food on the plate, he quickly grabbed half a sandwich and began to eat. He had to fight not to just shovel the food into his mouth. He never knew that a tuna sandwich could taste that good.

"I have my sister, who is my best friend." Cupid said, in between mouthfuls of his own food. "She runs the front of the store, while I do all the baking and food preparation. We have been talking about hiring someone to help me. Do either you or your brother know anything about baking or food prep?"

Peter quickly swallowed the bit of food in his mouth, wiping it with a napkin.

"I used to help in a coffee shop, but in the back like this." Peter sighed, thinking about how much he had loved that job. "I lost my job when we had to run."

"What happened? Why are you guys on the streets like this?"

Peter hesitated. It wasn't a story he shared with anyone, but Cupid was so open and trusting and it was almost as though the store welcomed him as he came through the door. "Our mom had been murdered," he whispered slowly, "and we didn't know where our father was. One night, the guys who killed our mom broke into the place to kill us, so me and my brother ran away."

"What are the police doing about all this? Surely, they have resources in place to help people like you?" Cupid demanded to know.

"The police have never helped us before, so we didn't bother going to them. The last time we tried, they told us to stop bothering them." Peter could still remember his meeting with the authorities and flushed with shame at the laughter he'd endured.

"Well, I can call my husband." Cupid smiled brightly. "He's a detective and he should be able to help you."

"I don't know if he can," The last thing Peter needed was more people looking into his life. "We're actually from a small town in Montana, and I don't think he can help since I assume he works here. Police jurisdiction and all that." Peter hoped he used the right words.

"Hmmm, I'll have to ask him. After sharing a story like that, I think we can both do with a drink." Cupid looked around the kitchen. "Ah, there it is."

Peter watched as Cupid got up and walked through an open doorway.

"I knew I had left some here." A smiling Cupid said, holding up a bottle of something.

"What is that?" Peter wasn't sure what was in the bottle, but when Cupid opened it, he smelled something sweet and alcoholic.

"This is my homemade brew." Cupid said, handing Peter a small amount of it in the shot glass. "I think you will like this, I found a great recipe for candy cane vodka."

Peter grabbed the glass and held it up to his nose. "It does smell really good."

Taking a small sip, he was surprised at how he wasn't able to taste the vodka, but he got a mouthful of sweetness.

"Oh," Peter moaned, "this is really good."

Slowly finishing his food, he kept sipping the drink until they were both all gone.

"So," Peter looked around, "where are the dishes I can help you with? But I must admit, I think I got the better end of the deal, that food was so good."

Cupid laughed, "It was a couple of tuna sandwiches. But fine, if you're sure, come this way."

The two men got up and Cupid led the way to the wash area.

"Here's where all the remains of my baking ends up," Cupid said with a flourish, indicating the sink area piled high with plates, bowls, and utensils of all shapes and sizes. "You can rinse the dishes here, and then they go into the industrial dishwasher. Have you used one of these before?"

Peter walked over and looked at the dishwasher.

"Yup, this is the same type the other shop had."

"Okay then," Cupid gave him another smile, "I'll let you get to work, and we can chat later about you possibly having this job."

Peter almost danced in happiness. "If you are happy with my work, I would love to keep coming back and working for you."

He could hardly wait to get back and tell his twin Harvey about their good luck.

Chapter Two

Peter looked around, then pressed his ear to the solid wooden door. One knock, a second one and then three quick taps. The third tap had barely finished when the door opened, and Peter was hauled inside. "Come see what I found for us," Harvey said with an excited grin. "Three cans of corn, whole cans, just a bit dented. I was so hungry, I ate the fourth can I found, but that was all, I promise. I wanted to share the rest with you."

"You're a good brother, Harvey." Peter let himself be pulled into a huge Harvey hug. At almost two feet taller and twice as heavy, his twin was a kind simple soul, who'd been crushed by the murder of their mother. When work proved hard to come by, his brother was always telling him he had to eat first, always teasing him about needing to grow more. As an adult, Peter knew he'd never grow any taller than his five foot four frame, and he'd always been skinny. Harvey took after their absent father, while Peter favored his mother. A mother he wasn't going to think about now.

"Look what I got for us," he said, pulling out of Harvey's arms and holding up the big paper bag. "I was scavenging for food in the dumpster outside that lovely smelling bakery, you know the one that always smells so good. Well, the owner caught me…."

"Did he hurt you?" Harvey growled. "If he hurt you…."

"No, no, no, nothing like that, I promise. Cupid is a good man." Peter was quick to assure his brother. "Look, he invited me in, gave me food in exchange for washing dishes. Even better, he says I can go back tomorrow. Harvey, I've got a job. Isn't that exciting?"

"A job?" Harvey's dark green eyes widened. "A real job, with regular pay and everything?"

"With regular pay and everything, although tonight he just gave me food. But Harvey, think about what this means…."

"We could save up," Harvey said excitedly, dragging Peter over to the overturned beer crate they used as a table. "We can save up and rent us a little house, small and out in the country…."

"Not too far," Peter warned with a laugh. "I still have to go to work and I don't want to walk miles to get there. But yes Harvey, we can finally have a small home of our own." Sitting his butt on the floor, he looked around at the warehouse office where there'd been staying. The entire block of warehouses had long been abandoned and squatters came and went in the huge expanse of space below. Peter knew the only reason they hadn't been ousted from the office, which offered them some semblance of privacy, was because of Harvey's meaty fists and growl. It was dark, cold at night and the tap in the corner constantly dripped. Peter looked at their two sleeping mats that offered little comfort against the concrete floors. "We can finally get a bed," he said. "Maybe even one each."

"Then we do have something to celebrate." Harvey beamed. But then his eyebrows came together. "You're going to be all right, aren't you? You didn't feel the need to shift, or get any bad vibes from that place. You know I can work. I just have to find someone…."

Peter's heart ached for his brother. Harvey was so sweet, but most people took one look at his size and were often scared of him. What was worse was the people who weren't scared of him – the ones who looked at his size and saw him as a challenge. Harvey trusted absolutely everyone and had been badly hurt in the past as a result. "Let me get settled in with my job," he said, patting his brother's arm. "Then maybe, I can ask Cupid if he knows of any construction crews hiring in the area. But honestly, I swear the place is fine. The bakery is even warded, did you know that?"

Harvey shook his head.

"I felt them as soon as I walked through the doors. They just tingled against my skin and then I swear it was like the walls were welcoming me. Isn't that strange?

"This Cupid is human?"

It was Peter's turn to nod as he pulled out the thick pack of sandwiches Cupid insisted he take, along with a half a dozen donuts and a couple of bottles of soda pop. "He's definitely human and I didn't get any sense he knows about the paranormal world the way he was talking. But someone very powerful is watching out for him. Who knows, because the wards let me in, maybe that same person can watch out for us too?" He could tell Harvey was undecided.

"We take each day as it comes, bro, remember?" Peter said gently, holding out one of the sandwiches. "I'm in no danger. Cupid is a really decent human being. All I'm doing is washing dishes there."

"Hmm," Harvey's mouth was full. It wasn't until he'd swallowed his huge mouthful, he said, "This bread is damn good, but it's not as good as yours. Why don't you tell Cupid you can actually cook? You know baking is your first love."

Peter's heart warmed under the praise. It was true, as soon as he stepped into Cupid's kitchen, his fingers had itched to start hunting for ingredients. But he wasn't going to reward Cupid's open heart or generosity by immediately demanding to be taken to the pantry. "I'm fine washing dishes," he said, picking up another sandwich. "Cupid runs the shop with his sister and I don't want to make any waves until they get to know me. Maybe once we get settled in a new home, I can ask him if I can help out in other ways."

"You're a better baker than he is," Harvey defended staunchly, and Peter grinned as he bit into his sandwich. His brother was biased although maybe his words were a smidgen true as well. Peter didn't care. He wanted to sleep. Tomorrow he could start his new job.

***

"I took on a new kitchen helper today," Cupid said drowsily, rolling into Liam's arms. It was late, the room still smelled of their lovemaking and even though Cupid knew he had to get up in a matter of hours, he took comfort in his husband's embrace. "I found him scavenging in my dumpster at the back of the shop."

"Why didn't you text me his name and contact details?" His sleepy partner was immediately awake. "I should check him out for you."

"There's nothing to check," Cupid laughed at his partner's formidable glare. It never fazed him. "The boy's name is Peter. He's homeless and struggling to feed himself and his twin brother Harvey. I got a good feeling about him and offered him the job. Athena agrees with me and it's a done deal."

"You should've just directed him to the shelter. That's what they're for," Liam grumbled.

"That was the first thing I did," Cupid chuckled and then his face dropped when he remembered what Peter told him. "Babe, those shelters are safe places, aren't they?" At Liam's quirked brow, Cupid went on to explain what Peter had told him. His heart sank at Liam's defeated expression.

"What can I tell you?" Liam shook his head. "The police are supposed to act on any complaint they get, regardless of who is laying the complaint. But we're under resourced and a lot of what goes on in the homeless community is ignored. The people who run the shelters do the best they can, but they can only control what goes on inside their walls. If this Peter of yours was threatened outside of the shelter, there's nothing they can do. Do you have any idea where the boys are staying? Perhaps I can talk to him, take him for a drive and get him to point the people out so we can keep an eye on them."

"He didn't offer the information and I didn't ask him," Cupid said. "He was ashamed enough of his situation as it was. I wasn't going to make it any worse. I'm just going to do my best to help him turn his life back around."

Liam was clearly thinking, and Cupid settled down to sleep. As much as he and his husband were connected in all ways, he couldn't and wouldn't deny the pull he felt to help Peter from the moment he saw him. It wasn't sexual, it wasn't even familial, but from the moment Cupid saw that mop of curls ducking in and out of the dumpster, he felt a connection – a strong driving need to help the proud young man. *Maybe I'll learn more about him when he trusts us,* Cupid thought as he closed his eyes.

Chapter Three

Peter knew he was early, but he was so excited to get to work. He was so very grateful that Cupid was willing to let him work, both for the money and the food.

Standing on the back step, he made sure he kept to the shadows. He knew he wasn't that close to the shelter, but he wasn't going to take any chances that someone could see him.

Harvey had walked him to work, not wanting him to be alone at the early hour. He had hoped that Harvey would wait and meet Cupid, but he insisted that he should leave. He was worried that he would scare Cupid.

Even though Harvey was the older twin, Peter felt responsible for him.

When they were young at the daycare that their mom had hired to look after them so she could work, one of the ladies had lost her patience with Harvey and had shaken him so badly that he ended up with some damage to his brain. Later, as it became more documented, they found out he suffered from *shaken baby syndrome.*

The money that was paid to them from the daycare allowed their mom to stay at home with them, but it was still tight. Once they were in school full time, their mom went back to work. Thankfully, since she was such a good nurse, the hospital she worked at was willing to give her the time off if she needed to look after them.

Hearing a noise, Peter looked up and saw Cupid walking towards him. Making sure to make some noise so he didn't startle him, Peter moved out of the shadows.

"Hey, what are you doing here so early?"

"Sorry, but I was just so excited to have a job that I could hardly wait to get here. I remember you saying that you were thinking about getting help for you in the kitchen, so I thought that I could possibly help you with a few other things too."

Peter was worried that he was assuming too much, but he really wanted to show Cupid that he could help him with whatever Cupid needed.

"Are you sure that you can work these long hours?" Cupid asked, a frown on his face. "I don't want you getting sick or hurting yourself working so long."

"Please," Peter was ready to beg. "I know what my limits are. I know I look small, but I'm a lot stronger than I look. Give me a chance to prove it to you?"

Cupid stood there, really looking at him.

"Okay," Cupid said after a moment. "I'm willing to give you a chance, but if it gets too much, you have to tell me. I don't want you wearing yourself out. That's a quick way to get sick or hurt."

"I promise," Peter swore to Cupid. "I will say something if it gets to be too much."

"All right, let's get started."

Cupid went and unlocked the door and turned off the alarm. Peter was once again surprised at the wards he could feel welcoming him into the shop. He wondered who set them, since Cupid really didn't seem to notice them at all.

"I usually start with making the dough for the donuts and pastries." Cupid said, moving around to get the mixing bowls and utensils ready. "I try to get them all ready and rising, then while that's happening, I will make the filling for the different items. The one that we sell the most are the turnovers with fruit fillings, followed by the donuts with fruit filling."

"Huh," Cupid tilted his head to the side. "I hadn't thought about it, but there sure are a lot of people with a sweet tooth."

Peter grinned at him, knowing that his brother had a crazy sweet tooth as well.

"I know what you mean. My brother could eat a whole tray of pastries all by himself. Mind you, he's about three times the size of me."

Cupid looked at him funny, "I thought you said you were twins?"

"We are, but not identical." Peter grinned at Cupid. "You should see the size of Harvey. Compared to me, he's ginormous!"

"Is that even a size?" A laughing Cupid asked.

"When you meet Harvey, you will agree that it fits him perfectly."

"I'm looking forward to meeting him," Cupid said, "but for now, we need to get to work."

"What do you want me to do first?"

"Grab the flour and let's make the donut dough."

As the two men worked, Cupid would keep giving him instructions, but he was already working on it. After they had the dough set aside, Cupid told him to go sit at the small table and brought them each a cup of coffee.

"I can see that you really do know your way around the kitchen. What was it that you did at your previous job?"

"I started out being the chef's helper, but when the chef was in a car accident, I stepped in and took over his duties. When it was determined that he couldn't return to work because of his injuries, the shop offered me the chef's position."

Peter leaned back in his chair, thinking about his former job.

"I really loved doing that, getting my hands in the dough and creating something that people would love to eat. Seeing their enjoyment at how the food tasted and looked was something that kept me motivated."

"Yeah," Cupid nodded his head. "I can understand that, as that's the same way I feel. Knowing that something that I made was making someone happy."

As soon as they finished their drinks, the two men got to work making the bread and the pastry dough.

Once they were set aside and rising, or resting, they began to make the donuts.

Cupid went over and made sure that the industrial sized deep fryer was full of fresh oil and heating to temperature.

"Do you also make bagels?" Peter asked.

"I do, but since they take so much longer to make, what I do is set aside a certain block of time each week and make enough that I can freeze them. I know that the bagels will keep in the freezer, but I prefer to make everything else fresh that day."

"I understand what you mean."

The men continued to work, getting most everything ready, when Cupid suddenly gasped in pain.

"What's wrong?" Peter hurried over to stand next to him.

"I misjudged where I had placed the knife and cut myself," Cupid said, hurrying over to the sink. He quickly turned on the cold water and was cleaning the area.

"Let me see." Peter said, as he gently grabbed Cupid's hand and studied the cut. "I don't think you're going to need any stitches, but you will need to keep your hand covered for a while. You went across the palm of your hand, so this could take some time to heal."

"Damn it, how am I going to work now?" Cupid groused out. "I can't close the shop."

"You don't." Peter calmly said. "You watch me work. I can follow your directions when it comes to the mixing and such, but you can do the filling. All you will need to do is wear a glove over your hand while doing it until it fully heals."

"You're right. I just hate not doing it myself."

"Ah, a control freak." Peter grinned at Cupid.

Cupid stared at Peter, then started to laugh. "Okay, maybe just a smidge."

The men snickered as they got Cupid's hand bandaged, and then while he went to get them each another cup of coffee, Peter finished getting everything ready for the baking ovens, or for the deep fryer.

"I have all the donut dough in the machine ready for you, so this way you can cook the donuts and I can handle the heavy trays in and out of the ovens." Peter told Cupid when he came back with their coffees.

"Wow, you really do know your way around the kitchen. I am so grateful I found you in my dumpster." Cupid grinned at Peter.

Both men jumped at the knocking they heard from the front of the shop.

"Oh, that's probably Liam." Cupid said, as he hurried to answer the door.

Peter smiled at Cupid, hearing the happy sound he made when he saw who it was.

"Hi babe." Peter heard a strange voice, guessing this was the love of Cupid's life.

"Come in, I want you to meet Peter." Cupid squealed with excitement.

"What happened to your hand?" Liam growled out.

"I accidently cut myself while working. It's a simple cut, but it's across the palm of my hand. Peter is helping me with the food prep and baking. He's been a godsend."

Cupid was saying all this as he was leading Liam back to the kitchen, so Peter was ready when they appeared in the doorway.

"Hi, I'm Peter Ames." Holding out his hand to Liam, he quickly shook it then looked up into his eyes. "I'm not trying to be rude, but I need to wash my hands again. I know that the first rule of cooking is keeping my hands clean, but I didn't want to offend you."

Cupid gave Peter a huge smile, while Liam just looked at him funny.

"You're so right." Cupid said. "I'm glad you take this so seriously, you have no idea how much I appreciate that."

"Sorry," Liam added. "I know how fussy Cupid can be about the food."

"Fussy!" Cupid glared at Liam. "I am not fussy! Food can be contaminated, look at Typhoid Mary. I'm happy that Peter takes this seriously and knows what to do properly."

Liam pulled Cupid into his arms. "You're right, and I'm sorry. Forgive me?"

Watching the kiss that they shared, Peter turned away to give them some privacy while he checked to make sure that everything was fine in the oven and the next trays to go in were ready.

"Go sit down, hun and I'll get you a cup of coffee."

As Liam moved to sit at the table, Peter looked over at him. "So, what would you like to know?"

Both men snickered at hearing Cupid laugh.

"Guess he knows me well." Liam said.

"I knew you would be coming by today to speak to me." Peter calmly said. "You're worried and since you don't know me, you want to make sure that Cupid is safe."

"You don't mind?" Liam thoughtfully asked.

"No, to me it shows that you love and care for him." Peter smiled this thanks to Cupid when he was handed a fresh cup of coffee. "I actually respect you for that."

So, while Peter and Cupid worked at cooking the food, they chatted. Peter left out nothing when he told Liam what happened before, and even about the guys from the shelter.

"Would you be willing to point them out to me?" Liam asked.

"I would, but can you make sure they don't know it was me?" Peter looked at Liam. "I don't want them to come after Harvey or me."

"I can do that." Liam sighed. "You know that I'm not going to be able to do much about the murder of your mom. You are right that because I work in a different city, hell a different state, that my hands are tied. I can't make them do anything they don't want to."

"Thank you, but that was what I had already guessed." Peter tried not to cry at knowing nothing would be done to those who killed his mom.

Cupid went to see Liam off, as he had to head back to the precinct.

Once he came back, the two of them worked happily, getting all the food ready for the day.

"How about I start on the dishes now, or do you want me to take out the trash first?" Peter asked.

"Let me worry about the trash. I still have a glove on my hand, so I can take the bags out. This way you can get started."

As Peter collected the dishes and put them into the sink, Cupid gathered all the trash and went out the back door.

"Peter! I think I found Harvey," Cupid yelled for him, the sound of fear in his voice caused him to drop the baking trays in the sink as he ran out the back door.

"Harvey." Peter cried out, running over the to huge man who was hiding behind the garbage bin. "What happened?"

Seeing how beaten and abused Harvey looked broke Peter's heart.

Chapter Four

The next few minutes were a mad blur of action. Harvey couldn't go into the kitchen, he was covered in dirt and mud and that was without the blood. Cupid offered his office, already on the phone to Liam, demanding someone come down and take action "right now." Quietly warmed by the passion Cupid was showing in his brother's defense, Harvey was all Peter could focus on as he led the stumbling man into Cupid's office space.

"Take a seat, tell me what happened?" Peter gently cradled Harvey's head. One side of his cheek was completely swollen, his eye half-closed and his lip bulging and split. What looked like rope marks braised his brother's neck and wrists and cuts seen through shredded clothing suggested a knife had been used. Only Harvey's hands and knuckles were free from injury.

"Bad men," Harvey moaned. "Bad men. They wanted to…."

"Did they… did they…?" Peter couldn't bring himself to say the word.

Harvey shook his head and then moaned again. "Wanted you. Wanted to know where you were. I didn't tell them. I didn't shift. I didn't…."

"Oh, fuck, Harvey." His eyes blinded by tears, Peter cradled his brother's head to his chest, taking care not to squeeze him too hard. "Who was it? Who did this?"

"I want to know that too." Liam's voice came from the doorway. "Geeze, man," he hurried over, "you need to be seen at a hospital."

"No hospital," Peter said quickly, too quickly, he realized when he saw Liam's frown deepen. "We don't have insurance, and we can't afford to pay."

"There's a clinic...."

Peter interrupted him. "Please, no hospitals, no clinics, no doctors. My brother's been through enough. They get him in there and they'll want to do tests, they might even take him away. Please."

Looking down, he stroked Harvey's matted hair, tears rolling down his cheeks. If Liam wanted to push the issue, Peter couldn't fight him. They'd have to run again, and Peter was tired of running. He had a job. He and Harvey finally had some hope for the future. He could hear Cupid talking in a low and urgent voice, and prayed the man was on his side. *Please, please, please, please, please.*

"Okay, no hospital," Liam sighed at last. "But man, I want to know who did this and when. You've got rope marks, you've been detained against your will and badly beaten. Why would someone do that to you?"

"Bad men." Harvey raised his head and growled. "Bad men want to hurt Peter. I didn't tell them. I didn't tell them where he was."

"Cupid, I'm so sorry. I'll, we'll have to go." Peter didn't stop his tears from falling. "I can't bring trouble to your place of work. I'm so sorry. This morning was the best time in my life in ages. Thank you so much for everything. Come on, Harvey."

"Neither of you are going anywhere." Cupid stood directly in Peter's path, his hands on his hips. "Your brother is hurt, you've got no place to go. If you think for one second, I'm turning you out on the streets when your brother is in this condition then you need your head examined. And besides, those apple turnovers you made are the best I've ever had, and they've sold out already. Now sit down both of you, and someone find a bloody first aid kit. It was in the kitchen last time I saw it."

"They'll come here," Peter protested. "We have to go. They probably followed Harvey. They could be here any minute."

"Then it's just as well I've got the police on my side." Cupid was not backing down.

"I'll call my brother, Aiden. He's on duty today and can bring a few friends," Liam said, pulling out his phone. "We'll set up a sting operation and catch them the moment they set foot in this store. But I want to know everything about these people, Harvey, is it? How many of them. Hair color, weight, height, approximate age. I want to know every freckle, mole, and any other identifying mark you can think of."

"Cupid," Athena ran into the office. "There're men at the counter. They're asking about Peter. They said they were friends of his."

"The only friends me and Harvey have are in this room." Fear gripped Peter's heart. Fear for his brother, fear for Cupid, his partner and his sister. Fear for the lovely store that would surely be wrecked if there was a fight.

"My brother is on his way." Liam straightened and stuck his chin out. "I'll go out and talk to them.

Harvey, I need you to try and peek and see if it's the ones who hurt you."

"It is them. I can smell them." Harvey's fists were clenched. "They won't take me unawares this time."

"Smelling them isn't part of police protocol when it comes to identifying perps." If Liam thought what Harvey said was strange it didn't show on his face. "Peeking, that's all, Harvey. I mean it. I just want a visual ID. Let the Police handle the rest."

Peter wasn't sure if it was Liam's alpha personality, or maybe Harvey's injuries were worse than they looked. A quick shift would cure most things, but it wasn't as though Harvey could do that until they were alone. Whatever it was, Harvey nodded, and relaxed his hands.

"Where can we see them without being seen?" Peter asked. He knew it was the same men who'd tried to catch him at the shelter. He knew the men waiting out front, sneering at Cupid's beautiful baking displays were the ones who'd hurt his brother.

"There's a hatch in the kitchen which would be the best place," Cupid sighed, looking at the mess Harvey was in. "Stuff it, we can just mop the floors and that sort of thing afterwards. Harvey, please try not to touch anything."

"I can't go in your kitchen." Harvey shrunk back. "Cleanliness is most important in food preparation areas," he recited slowly.

Giving his brother a quick hug, Peter said quietly, "That's very good, bro, but this time is a special exception, okay? We want these men to be caught, don't we?"

"Yes." Harvey looked puzzled. "What's a special exception?" He sounded the words out carefully.

"Like that time Mom let us have cake sitting on the couch instead of the table, because it was our birthday, remember?"

Harvey tried to crack a smile, and then winced as the split on his lip opened up again. "I miss our Mom," he said, his voice breaking up. "She'd make those bad men go away and leave us alone."

"I know, Harvey." Peter took a shuddering breath. "I miss her too."

"Hey," Cupid came around Harvey's chair and rested his hand on Harvey's knee. "You might not have your Mom anymore, but I bet wherever she is, she's looking down on you and smiling because she knows you have a new family now. Me, Liam, and Athena. You may think Athena is the quiet one, but believe me, you don't want to get on her bad side. She'd be out there with a baseball bat now if Liam wasn't here. You're not alone anymore, you wait and see. Things will only get better from now on. You have my word. Now come on. Liam can only stall those bozos for so long. Let's get you to the kitchen."

"He doesn't even know about us," Harvey whispered as Peter helped him to his feet. "Why would he say nice things like that?"

"Because they're good people," Peter replied. "And this is a good place. Can you feel it?"

"Makes my tummy tingle," Harvey agreed. "Let's go peek at bad men."

***

The small serving area in the Pantheon was packed with uniforms and scum bags. Peter watched as four men were taken away in handcuffs, cursing and swearing about their rights and being tricked. Liam was patiently coaxing Harvey to give his statement. Peter wasn't sure if Harvey would mention that the ringleader of the gang arrested hadn't been in the store. He made a note to mention it as soon as Liam was free.

Athena was busy cleaning Harvey's poor face and dressing his wounds when Cupid came over and motioned him to one side. "Look," he said firmly, "I'm going to be blunt about this. I know you're a proud man and you're doing all you can to keep you and your brother safe. But I want you here, working with me and you can't do that if you're worrying about your brother all day."

"I'm not giving up my brother," Peter said hotly. "I love being able to work here, but if it means…."

"Did I say that?" Cupid laughed. "You're as bad as I am, always jumping to conclusions. No, what I wanted to say is that I have an apartment on the floor above here. Athena used to live in it, years ago before she met her husband. It's got two small bedrooms with a shared bath. I know it's not much, but I want you and Harvey to stay in it, at least for the meanwhile."

A place of their own? Peter refused to let himself hope. "I don't have the money for the deposit, or first and last rent. We don't have any furniture…."

"The place is furnished already. It's basic but it has to be better than where you're staying now, right? It has hot running water."

Peter blushed, remembering how he'd explained to Cupid earlier how sick he was of washing himself under a cold tap.

"As for first and last rent, I'll deduct something from your pay each week to cover it. You'll have your own key. You and Harvey can come and go as you please. Is Harvey looking for work?"

"He does construction. He can fix anything," Peter said distractedly still trying to believe his good fortune. "But he needs someone…."

"Who understands how special he is," Cupid smiled. "I'm sure I can help find him a place. So, is it yes to the apartment?"

Peter wanted so badly to say yes, but life hadn't been kind and he hesitated. "Why us?" He asked quietly. "There's dozens of homeless people out there, all looking for a second chance. Why are you helping me and my brother?"

"Because you're the one who had the good taste to go foraging in my dumpster," Cupid said easily, nudging him on the shoulder. "So, I take it that's a yes. You can move in tonight. Oh, I'm sorry, we'll be closed for another hour or so," he called out to a tall, well-dressed man who peered around the door. "Please feel free to call again then."

"I was actually looking for the owner," the man said, his voice catching Peter's attention and holding it fast. "There was a disturbance in the wards...." He trailed off looking directly at Peter. "Oh no, oh no. The Fates did not just do this to me. I'm exempt, you bumbling fools." The man shook his fist at the ceiling.

"It's okay," Peter held up his hands, his feet urging him to move forward. He knew exactly what the handsome man was talking about. "I understand, you're rejecting me, and I can't blame you. Up until today I was a homeless nobody with no-one but my brother in my life. But please, even though I work here now, don't take away the wards. This is a good place and Cupid and his husband are good people."

"At least I know why the wards are all in a flux now," the tall man grumped. "I had no intention of removing them. I just wanted to ensure Cupid and Liam were safe."

"Do I know you?" Cupid asked, peering at the stranger. "I feel like I should. It's your eyes I think."

"We've never met in this form. But yeah, yeah, I'll increase the wards and make sure they're strong. For what it's worth, I'm sorry."

"Wait," Peter yelled as the intriguing man turned to leave. He grabbed the last box of apple turnovers he'd boxed before all the shit went down. Hurrying over to the man, he pressed the box into his hands. "Please take these. A small token. Something to apologize for me not being what you're looking for. I'm truly sorry. I quite agree you deserve so much better than me."

The man opened the box. "Apple turnovers," he whispered. "I haven't had these...." Abruptly he slammed the box closed. "Thank you. And please believe me when I tell you my rejection of you has nothing to do with your worth or otherwise. I just never intended to take a mate and I'm not doing it just because the Fates threw you in my path. You have a light, bright aura and a good soul. Be well." The door slammed behind him as the intriguing man left, taking the apple turnovers and Peter's heart with him.

"What the hell was all that about?" Cupid demanded. "Fates, mates and apple turnovers? You've got a lot of explaining to do young man. Did you know him? Our mysterious stranger?"

"No, I've never seen him before," Peter said quietly, before hurrying over to hug his brother.

Chapter Five

Peter quietly started to tell Harvey about the apartment, not wanting to speak yet of how his mate had rejected him. He knew the man wasn't a shifter, since he didn't smell like one. What he did smell was something amazing, like freshly baked bread and an apple turnover. Once he had a good whiff of him, he knew that he needed to give that box of treats to him.

He really wished he had a name for his mate. Guess it won't matter, since he wasn't wanted.

As they moved to go upstairs, Peter was having the hardest time trying not to cry out his pain. His other half wanted to shift and go find the man. Not even the loss of their mom had hurt this badly.

As Cupid showed them around, Peter took Harvey into one of the bedrooms and had him sit on the side of the bed.

"I'm going to go and get our clothes and other stuff." Peter told Harvey. "Why don't you go have a shower and get yourself cleaned up."

Looking around to see if they were alone, Peter quietly added. "and before you do, shift so you can heal your wounds."

"Can you help me take off my clothes?" Harvey asked. "I don't want to make them worse, and I should go with you. One of the bad mens wasn't caught."

"Yeah, I can help you. But as soon as you shift back to human, go into the shower."

"Okay Peter."

As the two of them worked at getting Harvey out of his clothes, without damaging them more, Peter kept telling him that being here was a good thing.

"Now, shift," he told Harvey.

Once Harvey was in his other form, he sat down on the floor and looked at Peter, tilting his head. He took a good sniff of Peter and when his eyes started to fill, Peter knew that he figured out something was hurting him.

Both men jumped at the yell they heard at the bedroom door, not realizing that Cupid was still in the apartment.

"What the hell." Cupid yelled out. "Where is your brother, and what is that?"

Cupid stumbled back when Harvey shifted back into his human form.

"What are you guys?" Liam asked, looking over Cupid's shoulder.

"Can Harvey go have a shower, and we can talk in the front room?" Peter calmly asked. Frankly, he was really surprised at how much Cupid and Liam weren't freaking out. He wondered if they did know about the paranormal world.

Once everyone was seated at the table, Peter took a deep breath, not sure where to begin.

"My brother and I are shifters, we are rare as I haven't heard of any other sasquatch shifters. It appears that our father must have been the shifter, since our mom was human."

"Wow, that must have been hard for her." Cupid added. "Wait, what…sasquatch. You mean you guys are bigfoot?"

"I prefer sasquatch, we are more than just bigfoot. And, I don't know if mom was upset about us being shifters, all I know is that she was our mom and loved us, unconditionally."

"Now I wish I had met her."

"She would have totally loved you." Peter smiled at Cupid.

"Now, I have a question for you two." Peter looked between Cupid and Liam. "Why aren't you freaking out?"

"I have to admit," Liam began, "that I've seen things in my line of work that I just can't explain. I've had things moved so that I can see them when I know they weren't there the first time I looked, and other stuff like that. One time I was chasing someone, and I saw that they were hit and knocked over, allowing me to catch them, but I never saw what knocked them over."

Cupid squirmed in his chair. "For me, I think it's because of our mom. I mean, look at my name! She always told us stories just before bed, and she made the whole idea of the gods and other stuff as real. I have to admit, it would be so neat to actually meet Cupid or Athena. Can you imagine meeting your namesake like that?"

"That would be so cool." Peter agreed. "Can you imagine what Olympus, or Valhalla would be like? Wonder what the real Thor looks like? Is he as hot as the actor?"

"Where is Thor?" Harvey asked from the doorway, "can I meet him too?"

"I'm sorry, Harvey." Peter got up and took Harvey's hand, pulling him towards the table. "We were just talking about if the gods were real, and if the god

Thor would be as hot as the actor who plays him in the movies."

"I don't know about the gods, but what other kind of paranormal is there out there that you guys know of?" Liam asked.

"Well, we know that there are other types of shifters out there. We haven't met any, but we have smelled wolves and foxes." Peter sat back in his chair, thinking about what else he may have scented.

"Rabbits." Harvey said. "I smelled rabbits and saw them once. They were really cute and fluffy. I told them they could play, and I would watch out for them. I think they were kids cause they were so small. A bigger bunny came and chased them off, I think it was scared of me. I would never hurt them, I promise."

Peter reached out and put his hand on Harvey's arm, "I know you would never hurt them, but I think everyone is scared of us when we are shifted. I guess we're kinda big."

"Kinda!" Cupid snickered. "I'm just lucky you didn't stand up, or we'd have to fix the hole in the ceiling."

Everyone snickered at that.

"I need to go to where we were staying and get our stuff. Cupid, can you stay here with Harvey and help him find a job?"

"I would love to help you Harvey, what do you like to do?"

"No." Harvey said. "Peter can't go alone, there is still bad mens out there."

"Harvey," Liam interrupted, "would you be okay if I go with Peter? I can drive him there and back and we can get your stuff quicker."

Harvey sat back, thinking about it.

"You promise to stay with Peter?"

"I promise." Liam said, lifting his right hand to hold over his heart.

"Okay," Harvey scowled at Liam, "but you better make sure he's home safe, or I'm gonna be mad at you."

***

"What is the source of that amazing smell?" Aletheia came bounding in, interrupting Cupid's snack. He quickly put a protective arm over the half-eaten box of pastries, glaring at his sister.

"Go away," he warned, showing his teeth. "This is mine, a gift, nothing for you."

"Oh, a gift," Aletheia sat across from him at the table. "You've got an admirer now? One who bakes? Aww, I've got it – it was Liam's Cupid wasn't it? Did he bake them for you?"

"Not my namesake, no." Cupid snuck his hand in and pulled out another turnover. "Someone he has working for him. Peter." Saying his name was a mistake. The damn Fates were canny when they twined two threads together. Just thinking about the sweet little man was enough to make Cupid's heart pound and his cock harden. What was worse, he knew Aletheia would pick up on it.

"Peter, hmm." Leaning over, Aletheia broke off half of the turnover in Cupid's hand. "There's something special about him. I can feel it in your voice. Come on. Spill. You know you want to."

"I don't want to do anything except enjoy my snack in peace." Cupid glared at the pastry going into his sister's mouth. She had no right stealing from him. Taking a bite of the remaining half, Cupid wanted to moan – again. Flakey pastry that melted in his mouth, soft gooey filling with just the right level of sweetness. Peter couldn't have known, wouldn't have known that apple turnovers were his favorite, but finding a good one, one that made him think of ancient days when times were simpler, and love was new, was damn near impossible. Peter had nailed it without even trying.

"Is this Peter of yours Bi?" Aletheia asked with a moan of her own. "Because I swear, if your fuck buddy can bake like this, I'd take him for a spin."

"He's not a fuck buddy," Cupid snarled shooting a mass of crumbs all over the table. Licking his finger, he carefully picked up every one and sucked his finger. "You will not go near him. You will not touch him. You won't even mention his name. Just leave him alone."

"If he's not yours then there's no rules against poaching him. Hmmm, that filling is just divine." Licking off her fingers, Aletheia eyed the box. "I'd let you shoot me with an arrow to have another one of those. Come on, tell me where I can find this Peter of yours."

"No, fuck you, I said NO." Grabbing the box under his arm, Cupid stormed out the room. Somehow the thought of Peter with his sister made him want to tear things up, smash some glasses, fucking shoot out firebolts instead of love arrows. Peter was innocent – that innocence shone in his soul. The thought of anyone touching him… Cupid growled, then found himself spun around by someone far bigger. So upset, he'd walked into Thor without realizing it.

"Hey, Cupid," Thor grinned. "Those baked goods smell divine. Can I have one?"

"No, you fucking can't and leave Peter alone you philandering bastard."

"Hey, I know who my parents are." Thor sounded aggrieved, but Cupid was beyond the apology stage.

"Just leave me the hell alone." Putting on a sprint, Cupid ran down the corridor to his own room. The wards welcomed him despite his anger. Closing the door, he carefully set the box on his bed. There was one pastry left. *Save it, eat it?* Cupid was torn. He hardly needed the pastry for nutritional purposes, but if he left it and saved it for another day someone might steal it. Cupid mentally cursed his sister and Thor.

But if I eat it, then that will be it. No more pastries. Somehow, that made Cupid's guts churn in a most unpleasant way. The box was from the bakery – keeping that wasn't going to soothe Cupid on those nights when he was too frustrated to sleep. And yep, Cupid knew that was coming. The Fates would push and push and there'd be nothing he could do but stay away from the one sweet man meant for him.

I could go back and get some more, Cupid reasoned with himself as his fingers reached out for the last pastry. *Peter doesn't have to be there. I could call, ask Athena to reserve some for me. I don't have to see him. I really shouldn't see him.*

Because Cupid knew Peter was a shifter and shifter's were hard wired to want no one but their mates once they'd scented them. *I'll give it a little while, then I'll find someone else for him. Someone worthy and kind, and who can look after him. I'll use my arrows. I'll make things right for him.* But as Cupid bit into the pastry, he was honest enough with himself to know that might take some time. Peter was far too special to let go to just anyone.

***

Aletheia knew there was something going on about Cupid and this Peter, and she knew just where to go to see this man. Her brother hadn't realized, but the logo for his namesakes' bakery was clearly visible on the box. She decided to go and see who this man was. Just for shits and giggles, she decided to take a friend with her. Thor would be perfect.

Chapter Six

Peter made quick work gathering what little he and Harvey had.

"Can I ask you a question?" Liam asked, and he helped throw their stuff into bags.

"Sure."

"Was your mom killed because of you being shifters?"

Peter stopped in shock, looking at Liam with his mouth hanging open.

"But no one knew!"

"Maybe someone found out, you said they did go back and try to kill you and Harvey."

Peter's legs gave out from under him and he fell onto the floor.

"We got our mom killed?"

"I don't know, but who are these guys that are coming after you now?" Liam wondered. "Could they be part of it, or just another set of assholes trying to take advantage of someone smaller than they are."

"All I can say is they don't smell the same as the ones who broke into the house." Peter stopped, giving Liam's questions some serious consideration.

"Thinking back to the night mom was killed and the night those guys came after us, the smell of them was similar, but different. The guys coming after me now don't smell like the others, but I'm not positive. We've been on the run now for months, so I might have forgotten their scent. I hope I haven't."

Liam gave him a sympathetic look. "I'm sure it's not easy, but your secret is safe with us. Cupid and I will never tell anyone about you two."

Peter sagged in relief. He was sure these guys were some of the good ones due to the wards protecting the shop, but it helped to hear the sincerity in Liam's voice.

"Thank you. I've been worried about finding a safe place for Harvey and myself. I know he wants to be working, so if you know of anyone who needs help, please let us know."

"One of the guys at work has a relative who works in construction, I'll make mention to him and see if we can get Harvey hooked up with them."

Peter was relieved to know that Liam may know someone. He was worried about who Harvey could end up working for and them being the wrong people for him to be around.

Standing up, Peter went over and grabbed a couple of the bags, and Liam grabbed the rest.

"Let's go home, I'm sure that Harvey is worried about me and Cupid is probably wondering where you are."

Liam started to laugh. "You don't know Cupid. Now that he has a new project, meaning getting your brother Harvey a job, he probably hasn't noticed that we're gone. Besides, if he can't help Harvey find a job, he'll just put him to work doing the dishes and such while getting you to help him with the baking."

"Well, I'm just glad that those guys haven't ruined Cupid's business. I was worried that they were going to some damage."

"That was why I'm glad it was near closing time that this all happened."

As they walked out of the warehouse, someone called out his name.

"Peter!"

Turning to look behind himself, he saw one of the older homeless guys who also stayed in the warehouse.

"Hey, Mark." Peter called out to him. "How can I help you?"

"I see you have all your stuff, do you mind if Saul and I take over your room?"

"Go ahead. I left behind the mats we had been using to sleep on, so you are welcome to them. I also left behind an old camp stove we found in the garbage. It's out of propane, but if you can get some, you can make some meals, and it will give you a bit of heat in the room too. I also left behind some old pots we found too."

"Thanks." Mark leaned in closer to Peter. "We sure are going to miss you guys, especially your brother. He made sure that no one messed with us. He helped to keep the peace."

"I'll be sure to let him know, and he's probably going to want to stop by and check up on you."

"He'll always be welcome here, he's one of the sweetest souls you can ever meet."

"Take care Mark, I need to get back to Harvey, so he doesn't worry about me."

"Give him our best, and good luck to you."

Liam paused and took a card out of his pocket, giving it to Mark.

"Stop in sometime and give this card to someone behind the counter. This will give you a free cup of coffee and a muffin."

Mark took the card, holding it carefully.

"Oh wow, this is for that coffee shop that always smells so amazing. Thank you."

"No worries, and besides, Peter here has a job there, baking in the back."

"I'm so happy for you two. I knew you didn't belong on the streets with us, you had homebodies written all over you."

"I know that you tried to keep Harvey safe when I wasn't around, and you have no idea how much I appreciated that. If I can, I'll try to stop by some evening with some left-over baked goods."

"Now that is something that we would love, thanks Peter. Take care of your brother."

Liam also pulled some money out of his wallet and handed it to Mark.

"Use this to get some propane, this way you can heat the room and cook some food. Get one of those barbeque propane cylinders from the gas station. If you all mingled your funds, you can buy some groceries and cook for a few of the others."

"Thank you, just wait till I tell Saul."

With a wave, Mark turned and went back into the building.

"Do you know why some of these guys don't go to the shelter?" Liam quietly asked.

"Some. Most of them were vets and because of the lack of treatment given to them, they are now on the streets. They no longer know how to have steady employment because of the years of mental abuse they have endured as homeless. I wish I could make it better for them, because most of them are really great people."

"I can see that, especially from the way they seemed to have looked after Harvey."

"Harvey wasn't always like this. Mom said he was fine, up until he was hurt at the daycare. That injury has left a permanent injury on his brain."

"What happened?"

"I guess these days it's called *Shaken Baby Syndrome*, and someone got frustrated with Harvey and hurt him. Guess what they called it didn't have a name until a few years later."

"I'm so sorry to hear that happened to him, he's such a sweet guy."

"He is, just don't try to hurt anyone around him and he won't have a problem with you, but the moment you do something to hurt another person or an animal, he will tear you apart."

Liam didn't say anything to that, and belatedly, Peter remembered who he was talking to. But as Liam drove them back to the bakery, and Peter and Harvey's new apartment, Peter was glad Liam was warned in a way. Harvey genuinely had a heart of gold. He rarely fought anyone who picked on him directly and was so happy if he came across a cute little kitten or a bunny rabbit, playing with them for hours if he could. But if he saw anyone smaller than him, and that was ninety percent of the population, getting hurt, he waded in to save the day. Never caring about his own safety, Harvey always wanted to protect others. Whether it was his shifter genetics, a result of being shaken as a child, or an innate part of who he was, Peter didn't know. But it was something he loved and respected about his brother, and if Liam and Cupid wanted to consider themselves family, then it was only right they knew too.

Chapter Seven

Cupid slammed down the book he was trying to read as a tingle ran down his neck. *Peter!* Someone was upsetting the wards around his namesake's shop – wards Cupid had intensified, strengthened and modified to allow the small shifter's energy signal to pass through. But whoever was passing through the wards around the shop now weren't just sauntering through them, they were smashing them.

Jumping to his feet, Cupid hesitated just for a second. Shifters became instantly attached to their mates – they couldn't help it. It was part of their make-up. Him seeing Peter would just upset the small shifter all the more, but…. The ward alarm felt more intense as they rattled down his arm for the second time. *Fuck it, it's a risk I have to take. I'm sorry little guy.*

Relocating in the alley behind the bakery, Cupid ran around and slammed open the door. What he saw made his blood boil and his fists clench. "What the hell are you two doing here?"

***

Peter had been surprised, and a little bit embarrassed when Athena poked her head around the kitchen door and told him a couple of customers wanted to compliment him on his baking. The previous night's sleep was the best he'd had in ages, curled up in a real bed. His hair was still all sticking out, because he'd spent so long in the shower, he didn't have time to dry it properly. Tugging on his clean t-shirt (he even had access to a washing machine), Peter looked across to Cupid for the okay before he left his post.

"Go on, Peter," Cupid smiled as he punched down some dough. "Your apple turnovers are selling as fast as you can make them. You deserve some recognition."

"It's your store," Peter mumbled, but with Athena waving her hand, and Cupid grinning like a loon, he didn't have much choice. Following Athena out of the kitchen, he stopped dead behind the counter. Standing there, as though coming to a bakery was an everyday occurrence were two of the finest looking beings he'd ever seen.

The woman was simply stunning with her long black hair falling in waves over her shoulders. Her form fitting dress discreetly clung to a frame that promised any straight man hours of pleasure. Her full lips were curled into a smile as she held out her hand. "Peter, we meet at last. My name is Aletheia."

"Do I know you?" But as Peter stepped forward to take the offered hand in his, he could scent the family tie to his mate. Bright eyes, just like his mate's, shone with amusement – something that did nothing for Peter's aching heart. Dropping her hand as quickly as he took it, Peter took a step back.

"My brother was given some delightful pastries yesterday and he was being so possessive over them, I just had to meet the man who created such wonderful goods," Aletheia purred. "Maybe when your shift finishes you could join me for a coffee?"

Peter didn't know where to look – his eyes darting around the room as he struggled to find a way to refuse gracefully. Yes, the woman claimed to be his mate's sister, but she was flirting with him and nothing about that felt right to him.

"Of course," a deeper voice sounded, coming from his side, "if Aletheia isn't your cup of tea, perhaps you'd consider dining with me instead?"

Muscles. Peter had read the phrase 'miles and miles of muscles before' but he'd never met anyone who filled that remark. Chest – Peter's head had to turn both ways to catch the full width of it. Biceps that definitely resembled basketballs if basketballs wore short sleeves.

Peering up, Peter stared at an inhumanly beautiful face framed by glorious wavy blond curls. He swallowed hard. *Oh man, if I wasn't mated, I'd climb him like a pole and hang on for the ride.*

But he was mated, at least in his eyes. Yes, the man in question had rejected him, and Peter would likely be alone for a very, very long time, but he wasn't the fickle type. He swallowed again so he could get the words out. "That's a no," even to his ears his voice sounded raspy. "No, thank you, to the coffee or the dinner, whoever you are." The muscled hunk had the same other-worldly scent his mate was carrying. *Maybe this hunk and his mate were lovers. Maybe that's why he rejected me.* Peter couldn't blame him if that was the case. This guy took the concept "drool-worthy" to a whole new level.

"My name is Thor," Thor's gray eyes twinkled. "I confess, Cupid wouldn't share your pastries with me at all, but they smelled divine. Are you sure you won't reconsider the dinner invitation?"

"Cupid!" Athena, who'd Peter had completely forgotten about, sounded shocked.

Thor chuckled in Athena's direction. "Your brother had to be named after somebody, didn't he? Yes, *that* Cupid is the one who took a gift box from this sexy young baker and stole his heart at the same time. It's written all over this poor darling's face. And seeing as the silly god couldn't appreciate the gift the Fates left for him, it's up to me to help this gentle young man find the will to love again – with me, this time."

"Wait... what... no." Peter stammered. "My kind only get one mate their entire lifetime. It's not possible to...."

"I have the Fates on speed dial," Thor confided leaning over the counter as if to get closer. "Cupid clearly rejected your bond, or you wouldn't be here, with your aura all pale and sad."

"Well, yes, but..." *Someone come in, please. Someone human, normal, someone who just wants to buy donuts or something, Please.*

As if in answer to his pleas, the front door of the bakery flew open, but it wasn't the normal human customer Peter had asked for. Cupid, the god this time, stood framed by the door, his fists clenched, his scowl etched deep on his face. "What the hell are you two doing here?"

Chapter Eight

Cupid was beyond pissed. How dare they even speak to his mate. Okay, it was the mate he rejected, but that was irrelevant. These two predatory assholes had no right going near Peter for any reason.

"Well, is someone going to explain this to me?" *I can't look at Peter. Focus.*

"It's very easy, dear brother. Thor tells me Peter is your mate. Peter confirmed it. You rejected him, which was a shitty thing to do. Now, Thor and I are willing to help him find a mate. Someone who will appreciate him."

"You don't get to decide that." Cupid snarled out. He moved so that he was closer to Peter, even if he couldn't look at him. No one was getting their hands on him.

"Really." Thor drawled out, reaching out his arm and wrapping it around Peter across the counter. "I'm sure that the fates had a better mate in mind for this little cutie. How they could've even considered you is beyond my comprehension."

Cupid watched as Peter tried to pull away from Thor. Stupid Norse god better be thankful that the counter was still separating them.

"What's going on here?" Liam's voice was heard from the doorway. "What are you doing here in my husband's shop?"

"Um, Liam" Athena said, moving closer to him. "These are the real gods. The beautiful blond is Thor, and over there is Cupid. I'm not sure who the lady is, but if she is his brother, then she is Aletheia."

"Very good sweets." Aletheia purred. "You have made your namesake proud, she was always impressed at your ability to keep others safe."

"I...but...really?" Athena stammered out.

"Enough." Cupid roared out. "Thor, get your damn hands off Peter."

"This isn't the same Cupid I'm used to from the books Mom read to us." Cupid said, peeking into the room from behind Liam.

"Can you please let me go?" Peter asked Thor.

"It's okay sweetheart, once we get this sorted out with the Fates, it'll be all good." Thor smiled down at him.

"I'm going to fucking kill you if you don't get your hands off Peter." Cupid snarled out.

"Wow," Cupid whispered out. "He sure is cranky." Cupid looked up to his husband.

"I'm not sure what's going on, but can you step back into the kitchen?"

"No." Cupid snorted out. "This is much more fun."

"What the hell is going on here." Athena yelled out. "You don't get to come in here and create this kind of havoc."

Athena walked up to Peter and pulled him away from Thor.

"I don't give a shit how hot you look, you're scaring Peter." Athena wrapped her arm around Peter and led him over to the kitchen doorway so Cupid could look after him.

As soon as he left, Athena turned around and stomped over to the original Cupid.

"What the hell can I call you, so I don't keep confusing you with my brother?"

"If you want, you can use the Greek version of my name, Eros." Worrying about names was the last thing Cupid/Eros wanted to think about.

"We can always call you asshole, since you are rejecting your mate." Thor snarled out. "Peter is one of the sweetest men, and you turned your back to him."

"I don't have time for a mate." Eros yelled back.

Everyone turned when they heard a howl of pain coming from the kitchen, followed by Cupid yelling.

When everyone tried to get into the kitchen, they found the way blocked by Athena.

"No, you don't get to go back there."

"That's my mate."

"No, he's not." Athena snapped back. "Since you have rejected him, then you don't get to see him. We are now his family, we'll look after him."

"Can I help too?" Aletheia asked

"You all can leave, you've hurt him enough." Cupid snarled out from behind Athena. Stepping around her, he faced the three gods head on.

"I don't give a howling hoot where you came from, or who you are." Cupid kept walking towards them, causing them to keep taking a step back.

"You have hurt my friend. Someone who never hurt any of you." Cupid pointed towards the kitchen. "He's in there, falling apart because his mate is an asshole. I don't know what happens to shifter's who have been rejected, but I swear to all that's holy, if anything happens to Peter because of you, I will find a way to make you regret it."

Stepping around the three gods, Cupid opened the door and pointed out it.

"Now, get your asses out of here, and don't come back until you make things right for my friend."

After saying that, Cupid slammed the door in their faces and locked it.

"He does realize that we can just walk back in there?" Thor quizzically asked.

"I'm sure he does, but I won't do that." Aletheia said. "I admire him, standing up for his friend."

"Yeah," Thor nodded, "I do too. He's got one hell of a set of balls, standing up to us like that."

"True" Aletheia agreed. "So, Eros, do you know what happens to shifters who have been rejected by their mates?"

"I imagine it depends on the shifter type. I don't have a lot to do with them, as they already have their senses to guide them to when a mate is near. Why do you ask?" Eros looked at his sister from the reflection in the glass as he kept looking into the store.

"Well, I'm pretty sure that within a few days, a week at most, Peter will fade away."

"What, no." Eros scoffed. "You've been listening to urban myths. He might be small in human terms, but he has a powerful shifter inside of him."

"Check back on him tomorrow, then let me know. I haven't got a problem with telling you, I told you so."

After dropping that bomb, Aletheia and Thor disappeared.

***

Heart...broken, can't breathe. Peter was in agony, his mate had rejected him, but this time, it was in front of witnesses.

Shattering like a cartoon heart into a million tiny dust particles, Peter realized in a sudden moment of clarity, there was nothing left for him. His dreams of a home, someone to love him for all time, care for him, and work with him were torn to pieces with the slam of the bakery door. It was as if he was frozen, terrified that if he moved so much as an inch, his entire body would fall apart.

Staring down at the floor, Peter didn't even see it, his mind had been repeating the scene where

Cupid/Eros rejected him. *I don't have time for a mate.* Gods, those simple words drove a knife through Peter's core being. His animal whimpered – they weren't a chore. A mate wasn't something that had to be made time for, mates just clicked, and their lives fit together like two pieces of a puzzle. How could Eros reject him without even trying – how could he be so public about it?

Harvey picking him up and carrying him to bed didn't register. Cupid, was it Cupid who undressed him and put him under the covers? Peter didn't know or care. All he knew was no matter how strong he'd tried to be when his mother died, strong for himself and for Harvey, in that moment he was completely drained. All he wanted to do was cry until his body turned to dust and he ceased to exist. Replaying the scene of his rejection in an endless loop in his mind, Peter never even felt Harvey get on the bed and wrap him up in his arms, crying with him.

Chapter Nine

"Explain to me about this mating business," Cupid said firmly, setting a tray on Harvey's lap, putting the fork in his hand. Peter appeared to be sleeping although his breathing was really shallow. Twenty-four hours after his breakdown, the poor boy had barely moved. Harvey refused to leave his side except to use the bathroom. "Now come on Harvey, I know your brother would want you to be strong for him, but tell me what we're dealing with here. Why is this mates thing so important? Is it because you can turn into Sasquatches? Do I need to call a doctor for him?"

"No doctors," Harvey shook his big head. "Doctors can't help mate sickness."

"Mate sickness?" Liam had a notebook in his hand. "Is this a medical condition among your kind?"

Harvey shook his head again. "It just happens." He prodded at the pancakes Cupid had made for him, but didn't eat.

"Harvey, come on," Cupid implored. "You can't get sick too. You need to eat, keep your strength up for when Peter wakes up." When Harvey still didn't make a move to eat, Cupid had an idea. "If you clear that plate, I'll let you play with my cat and kitten."

"You have a kitty?" Harvey cut into his pancake with the fork and took a mouthful. Cupid shared a look with his husband, breathing a sigh of relief.

"I have a kitty named Special Kitty and a cat called Hellcat. You can meet them real soon. But I need to know what's happened to Peter. Why won't he wake up?"

Chewing slowly, Harvey swallowed hard. "He might never wake up." Big fat tears rolled down his cheeks. "When one of us meets our mate, it's a wonderful thing. My mom told me. Your senses come alive, your mate is the most wonderful thing you've ever smelled before. You get super horny and want to have sex with each other all the time."

"Sounds like us, babe," Cupid smiled softly at his husband. "Go on, what else can you tell us about mates?"

"They fit," Harvey said simply, looking at the wedge of pancake on his fork. "If one person is angry about something, their mate can make them calm. When one of them is sad, the other one makes him feel better. If one of them is hurt, the other one is so protective and cares for them, and makes sure no one can hurt their mate again. Mates don't cheat, they don't lie to each other, and they always put their mates first in everything."

"That does sound wonderful," Cupid said, prodding at Harvey's arm to encourage him to eat again. "But there's one thing I don't understand. Peter met Cupid, Eros or whoever the hell he was the day before. He gave him a box of apple turnovers, but he didn't just collapse on the floor and not move when the guy left."

"He didn't tell me." Harvey looked over his shoulder at his motionless brother. "He wouldn't want me to worry about him. My guess is Eros only rejected him personally then. Maybe Peter thought he'd change his mind and come back later. But this time, Eros told everyone. There's nothing more final than that." Putting down his fork, Harvey burst into loud wailing, tears streaming down his cheeks. "He's going to die."

"Oh no, Harvey, he won't die. We won't let him die." Scrambling closer, Cupid wrapped his arm around Harvey's huge shoulder, patting his head as Harvey's wails grew louder. Looking helplessly at Liam, who was as broken up as he was, Cupid mouthed *What on earth are we going to do?*

***

"Meh." Eros sighed as he raised his arm, letting a small arrow fly across the nightclub. It hit his mark, just as Eros knew it would, causing the hopeless man to see his date for the evening in a whole new light. Normally Eros got a burst of happiness knowing another immortal connection had been made. Love had been in short supply for years, and yet one by one, couple by couple, Eros was fighting hard to stem the tide of hate.

Rubbing his eyes, Eros turned back to the bar, lifting his finger for another drink. He felt like he hadn't slept properly for months. Every time he laid down, his eyes barely staying open, his head was plagued with call after call as humans pleaded, begged and cried out for someone to love them. *It never ends,* he thought hopelessly.

"You look like shit." Aletheia appeared at the bar beside him. "Have you been to see your mate yet?"

"I'm working." Refusing to even look at his sister, Eros leaned his back against the bar, scanning the crowds. His mark for the evening had already been hit, but sometimes Eros caught sight of other connections that needed a helping hand. Eros was happy to help them too. Anything to stop the incessant clamor in his head.

"Cupid, Eros, you can't be that stupid," Aletheia hissed. "It's been four days. Thor and I have been checking on him, but there's nothing we can do. He's fading."

Suddenly, Eros was angry, really angry. Uncaring if anyone noticed, he grabbed his sister's arm and translocated them out into the alley behind the club. "You do not get to call me stupid and I'm sick to death of you acting like a drama llama. You have no idea what my job is like. There are thousands, literally thousands of humans begging to the cosmos, desperate to meet the love of their life. Their calling keeps me awake at night. I could zap around from place to place twenty-four seven for the next fifty years and I'd never reach them all. Why? Because for every person who I do make a match for, a dozen new ones take their place. Don't you get it. I. Don't. Have. Time. For. A. Mate."

"So, you'll let your mate die, just so others can find the love you long for?" Aletheia shook her head. "You know more than anyone the story of Fated Mates. Peter only gets one, and you're it."

"He'll get over it. He's got his brother to look after." Eros knew the words were weak even by his standards. "You don't understand how important my job is."

"I do know how important your job is," Aletheia would not back down. "I can only imagine that's why the Fates sought to bless you with a mate when the rest of us don't have one. You more than anyone need the support a loved one can bring. And as for getting over it, get over yourself. Fuck it, go and see him if you don't believe me. Cupid is ordering Harvey a black suit as we speak."

Eros felt a pang of doubt. He'd been so sure Peter would recover and move on without him. "I read up about shifters. They only die if they've claimed their mate and something happens to one of them. Peter and I have barely said five words to each other."

"You damn fool," Aletheia's punch was going to leave a bruise on his arm. "Shifters know their mates by scent. Peter scented you. His animal half knows you're his mate and accepted you instantly. Now you've rejected him in front of witnesses. That poor beast is going to pine away and take Peter with him."

"You'd better not be joking with me," Eros warned, knowing he was going to have to check. "If I go back and see him up and about acting as though nothing's happened, I'll… I'll…." Eros couldn't think of a threat harsh enough – one of the joys of having god-like siblings.

"The next time you see me, you'll have some of those apple turnovers as a gift to me, to say thank you, for not letting that poor man fade away because you were too thick to see how good things could be between you. Now, get on. Go to him, and pray you're not too late."

Chapter Ten

Cupid/Eros waited until there was no one in the room, then quietly moved into it.

Aletheia was right, his mate was near death, and it was his fault.

"Why did you mate me with this man?" Eros softly snarled, glaring at the ceiling. "You had to know how bad it's gotten for me, the incessant cries of the lonely. Why would you do this to Peter, he doesn't deserve this."

"Because he's as lonely as you are, but he's also as loving." Atropos said, appearing in the dimly lit room, her sisters on either side of her. Eros would gape, the Fates were rarely seen by anyone, but he was too busy listening to the woman justify herself. "He would be the perfect person to be at your side, helping you, supporting you."

Shaking her head, she moved away from her sisters and went over to the bed to brush a gentle hand over Peter's brow.

"And now, I'm about to cut his thread, well before it was his time."

Eros watched as a tear slipped down her face, only to fall onto the bed.

"Then you are making that choice. You can't put that on me. Why can't you mate him with someone else?" Eros begged. "If he's so loving then mate him with someone who will love him like he's meant to be loved."

"That someone is you." Lachesis said firmly. "Peter has a light in his soul that few share. His past experiences would have rendered any other man bitter and twisted, but not him. All he's ever done is try and watch out for his brother and work to keep them both safe. He deserves the grandest kind of love and who better to give that to him than the god of love himself?"

Eros moved his head, intending to glare at the remaining two sisters, when he saw what was in Clotho hands.

"What are you doing?" He cried out.

"Fixing what you are destroying with your foolishness." Clotho calmly said.

Eros tried to get up and move away, but he was held in place by an unseen force. He watched in disbelief as Clotho pulled back on the bow and shot him with one of his arrows.

Peter felt like he was trying to walk through mud. He could feel that someone was calling to him, needing him, but he had no idea who. All he saw around him was mud, trying to suck him down into it.

"Please, Peter, wake up." The voice said. "I'm here, my mate, please come back to me."

Mate, hang on, his mate rejected him. Who would be calling him mate?

"You need to wake, young Peter." A woman's voice softly said.

Turning towards the voice, he saw three women, standing together. He turned and walked to them as fast as he could. The closer he got, the less the mud was sucking him down. When he finally got near them, he found he was able to walk on solid ground.

"Who are you?" Peter asked them, "where are we?"

"We are the Fates. I am Atropos, the older sister." She held out her hand to Peter and when he grabbed it, he felt comforted by her, like when he held his mom's hand.

"Thank you for that lovely compliment," She said.

"You can read my mind?"

"Of course, we are the Fates," The middle aged woman said. "I am Lachesis, and this is Clotho." Lachesis pointed to the youngest looking woman.

"Hi." Peter looked at them. They were all beautiful in their own way, but what he appreciated more was the feeling of calm and love that emanated from them.

"Where are we?" Peter again asked, looking around and now seeing a forest growing out of the mud.

"We are in your mind, young one. We are here to help you back to the land of the living, back to your mate."

"What mate?" Peter aimed for a dismissive tone, something hard to do when his heart still hurt from what Eros had done. "You mean the one who publicly rejected me. I'm not going back."

"Ah, but there has been a change in him." Lachesis said, with a smile. "I don't think you'll find he'll reject you any more."

"What do you mean?" The women might be beautiful and powerful in their own right, but that didn't mean he wouldn't be suspicious of them or their motives.

"Have no worries, young Peter." Atropos said, as she wrapped her arm around his shoulders. "We just helped Eros along. He would have come around in due time, but when you began to fade, we had to step in."

"What have you done to him!" Peter asked in horror. Fading hurt, being in the depths of despair was equivalent to traipsing through the mud in his mind, but Peter never, ever wanted anything to harm his mate.

"We gave him a dose of his own medicine." Clotho giggled. "I shot him with one of his own arrows."

"Why would you do that?" Peter couldn't believe what he was hearing. "Why force him to be with me, when that's not what he chose for himself. How can you even think that's how I wanted to be with my mate. If he wanted me, he would be by my side by his choice, not your trickery."

"He will be with you, because that's what he does want deep inside," Atropos said. "The arrow only helps him to see what is in front of him. Give him the chance to prove it."

"If it doesn't work, and Eros can't be the mate you need," Lachesis added as Peter was still busy trying to work out when his life had gotten so complicated, "then call on us and we will help you by attaching your string with another mate."

"We aren't cruel. We truly believe Cupid, or as you call him, Eros, is the man for you." Clotho added, "We do sometimes make mistakes, but they are very rare."

"Go back to the living, please?" Lachesis asked.

Peter stood quietly for a moment, staring off into the distance. *Dare he give Eros another chance? Could he handle his heart being broken again?* Peter thought about Eros, the gorgeous god who spent all his time finding love for others. Was it possible the god had spent all this time alone? Instinctively, his heart immediately warmed to the god. *Maybe there was a good reason for his rejection. I never thought to ask.* And then Peter thought of Harvey, and Cupid and Liam, and how they'd tried to help him turn his life around. Was he really going to throw it all away, when the opportunity for true happiness lay just beyond his reach?

Heaving a sigh, Peter turned and nodded his head to the three Fates.

"Okay. I'll try." He looked around, wondering how to get back.

"Allow me," Atropos said, suddenly giving him a hard push.

Suddenly Peter was back in his bed. He sat up with a gasp. Eros was there slumped in a chair by the bed, his face filled with sorrow, his clothes rumpled as though he'd slept in them.

"Eros?" Peter's mouth was so dry he could barely get a word out. He ran his tongue around his teeth, trying to get some saliva moving. "Are you all right? Clotho said she shot you."

"It's good to see you awake," Eros's smile, while strained still contained enough warmth to send a flutter through Peter's heart. "Clotho did shoot me with one of my own arrows. Kinda ironic really. Here, let me get you some water." A glass appeared in Eros's hand and the man himself came over, holding it for Peter while he took a few grateful sips.

"Ironic how?" He asked, when his mouth and throat felt less like a desert floor.

Taking the glass back, Eros looked thoughtful. "I've always heard," he said at last, "that when hit by one of Cupid's arrows, the person hit feels a state of euphoria. It's as though the arrow clears away all the noise that might have stopped them getting into a new relationship, and they can truly see the connection between themselves and the other person. I've seen it myself thousands of times. It's such a happy and wonderful moment for both parties and sets them up for the love that will last their whole lifetime."

"I don't see anything ironic about that." Peter had a horrible thought. "Wait, are you saying the arrow didn't work on you?"

"That's exactly what I'm saying." Eros scratched his chin. "Makes sense in a way. I can't tell you how many arrows I misfired when I first got this position.

Peter failed to see any possible humor in a god of love shooting himself in the foot. He was too busy wondering why the hell he'd let the Fates talk him into coming back. His animal half wanted Eros. Splicing another thread to his wasn't going to change that.

"Of course," Eros continued, "maybe I didn't feel affected by the arrow because I already knew how strong the connection was between us."

Okay. Now Peter was confused. "You saw the connection but rejected me anyway?"

"I thought I had to." Agitated, Eros got to his feet and started pacing the floor. Peter could appreciate the flex of a decent pair of legs as well as the next man, but he was more worried about what might come out of the man's mouth.

"I don't think anyone appreciates what it's like to be me," Eros said, waving his hands in the air. "You know all those times when someone wishes they had someone to love? Well, guess who hears them? Me! And do you know how many people voice that wish? Thousands and thousands of them, every single day."

"That must be very noisy for you." Peter wondered how Eros heard all those people. Did he get voice messages on his phone or something?

"I love my work, don't get me wrong," Eros stopped by the side of the bed and fell to his knees. "Bringing two people together who might otherwise have missed each other is an awesome feeling."

"But," Peter prompted, resisting the urge to run his fingers through Eros's curls.

"But those connections could or would have been made anyway if those humans would just get their noses out of their phones long enough to look around them." Eros pressed his forehead into the mattress and groaned. "Work mates who are destined to be together. Best friends, people who've known each other for years.

Their love connection is right there under their noses and they don't even see."

"Maybe people are scared to look at their friends or co-workers like that." Peter had always thought Cupid was the one responsible for two strangers, whose eyes meet across a crowded room and then bam, they form a love connection. "It's not an easy thing to do, declaring feelings for someone if you're worried about being rejected. Feelings can make someone feel really vulnerable if they're expressed, you know, publicly."

"You really believe that?" Eros raised his head.

"Of course. Look," Peter warmed to his theme. "Things aren't like they used to be in the olden days. There're a lot more people concentrated in one area for a start. And then there's the laws protecting you from aspects like workplace harassment for example. I mean, what if a guy at work professed his feelings for a lady he worked with and she sued him for harassment? That guy would probably spend months stalking his lady on social media, before he even mentioned something casual like, 'will you have coffee with me.' Then there's the fact everyone's so busy – work and money focused. Someone could be sending them all the right signals, and they're just too busy to notice it. I think what you do is an amazing thing, because underneath, everyone wants to be loved. It's like your arrows give them the strength and confidence to act on their feelings."

"Wow. Er... thank you." Eros looked shocked by the compliment. "I guess the Fates were right. You do have a way of making me feel better about things."

"Yeah, well, it doesn't mean you have to stay with me." Peter looked down at his hands. "I couldn't help what happened, to me I mean. My animal half is a lot bigger than me, but he doesn't get a lot of love from others, except Harvey of course. I mean, it's not like I'm a wolf, or one of those exotic cat shifters or something that people want to get close to. But just because I'm big and hairy-looking doesn't mean I don't want someone to hug me sometimes. My animal took one sniff of you and he was hooked."

"What kind of animal spirit are you?" Eros looked embarrassed just asking. "I don't have a lot to do with the paranormal world. They can find their mates quite happily without my interference."

He has to know sometime. Inhaling sharply, Peter said, "I'm a sasquatch. My brother, Harvey is one too."

"Get out of here, you're kidding me." Eros's eyes looked as though they were going to fall out of his head.

"No, I wouldn't joke about something like that," Peter said hotly. "Yeah, I know we're not all arrogant and aristocratic like wolves, and I don't purr like a pussy cat, but there's nothing wrong with who I am. My shifter half has beautiful fur and he always keeps it clean. He doesn't smell bad or…."

"Woah, woah, woah." Eros put up his hands. "I wasn't judging you. I'm thrilled to bits about it."

"You are?" Any anger Peter felt at being judged slipped away.

"Hell yes." Eros shook his head as he smiled. "Do you know how long I've waited to meet one of your kind? You're like the supernatural stars of the supernatural. I'm freaking thrilled. Do you think you could shift for me sometime?"

Peter's stomach took that moment to grumble. He couldn't remember the last time he'd eaten anything substantial. "You do know it means I'll have to get naked and I should probably eat something first."

"I can do food," Eros waved his hands and the bed was covered with a large lap table full of covered plates.

"Wow, I bet that comes in handy sometimes." Peter decided to push his luck a little further. "Does this constitute our first date?"

This time Eros's grin held a wealth of sexy promise. "We have food, a bed, and you've already said you'll get naked with me. I'd say it's the best first date ever."

Chapter Eleven

Eros was pleased to know that he was providing for his mate, even though all he had to do was wave his hand. Watching Peter eat the food made him feel good.

"Please, I'm not going to eat all this, so have some." Peter's large chocolate brown eyes were doing amazing things to him.

"How about you eat what you can, and I'll nibble with you?"

The smile that Peter gave him melted him, and he knew that he would give up his single status tonight. After tonight he would be a mated man. Something he'd never envisaged, but now he embraced the idea.

"I'm curious about something," Peter started. "If you are a god, and I'm a mortal, what happens to you when I die?"

Eros frozen. "Umm, I don't know."

"Who do we ask?"

"Atropos!" Eros yelled at the ceiling. The Fate's face looked eerie against the off-white paint. "What is the answer?"

"Really, you should know this." Atropos's ghostly visage shook her head at him. "When the two of you mate, your life thread, Peter, will be matched to Eros's. Meaning you will not die so long as he is alive. We'd never weave a couple into the tapestry and then cut only one of them short." She disappeared.

"What…? I mean, knowing I won't die early and cause you any pain is a good thing, right. But what about Harvey." Peter looked to him with tears in his eyes. "I'll have to live without my brother? I'll have to watch him die, just like my mother?"

"Oh, my mate," Eros got up and went over to wrap his arms around his quietly shaking mate. "We still have a long time yet before that happens, and we can figure it out by then."

"Promise?" Peter sniffled.

"I promise. I know how important Harvey is to you."

"Thank you. He's my only family, other than you."

Eros was humbled that Peter included him as part of his family, considering how he had been treated by him until now.

"I promise to do everything I can for him, but in the end, the choice will have to be his, and his mate's."

"I know," Peter sighed, "but I want to know that the option to not lose him might be there."

As Peter moved the food around on his plate, Eros was able to hear his stomach let out a bunch of small growls.

"You know," Eros drawled, "if you don't eat more, we won't be able to get to the claiming part of the evening. You've not been eating, you need to build up your strength."

He had to laugh, Peter sat there watching him with an almost feral look in his eyes as he began to eat as quickly as he could. Once he had the plate cleaned off, Peter put it on the bed, then grabbed a napkin and wiped his mouth. Eros had a hard time not just leaning down and licking him clean. He really wanted a taste of his mate.

"Eros." Peter reached out a hand and cupped his cheek, saying with all seriousness. "I really need you to get rid of all this food now. I imagine you fucking me through the mattress could be awkward with plates and crumbs in the way."

Oh, my gods, I can't believe he just came out and said that. Eros thought he might have to revise his opinion of Peter being a sweet and innocent young man.

But he was hardly going to ignore his mate's request. With a wave of his hand, the bed was cleaned off, not a single crumb left behind.

"How long have I been in bed for?" Peter asked him, nervously nibbling his bottom lip.

"It's been a couple of days, why?"

"I would really like a shower and to brush my teeth." Peter looked embarrassed. "As much as I want to belong to you, I would prefer if I didn't feel so dirty."

The idea of Peter being dirty from what Eros wanted to do to him, had his blood heating in Eros's veins.

"You do know that I can fix that for you, this way we can get to the fun part of the evening." Eros growled out. "Then once I have you all dirty from the things I'm doing to you, we can shower and get all clean, just so we can start over again with the getting dirty."

Eros moved so that he was leaning over Peter, with his hands on either side of Peter's head. He leaned down, getting nose to nose with his sweet shifter. Now that he decided that he wanted to be with his mate, Eros was done waiting.

"I want to tease you, lick you, and take my time tasting every inch of you." Eros whispered into Peter's mouth. "Once I have memorized every inch with my tongue, I plan on slowly getting you ready for my cock. I'm going to take my time stretching you, so you are wide open and ready for me."

Eros watched as Peter's eyes dilated, until they were almost all black. He was panting, as if he had run a marathon. The whimpering noises coming from Peter were driving him crazy, and when they finally mated, Eros wanted to hear him scream in pleasure.

With another wave of his hand, he had them both naked, and he made sure that Peter felt nice and clean. He was so ready for them both to get messy again.

"Oh my god." Peter groaned. "You're making me crazy."

"I've only just started, so I hope you're ready."

"Please...I need you."

Eros could hear the desperation in Peter's voice, see it in his eyes. He knew that he felt the same way. Worried that this was going to be the shortest mating in history Eros decided taking the edge off might be best for both of them.

"I have you." Eros said, as he moved to lay on top of Peter.

Holding himself up with one arm, Eros moved his other hand so that he could hold both of their cocks together. Peter jumped and then relaxed into his hold.

"Let's take the edge off, then I can take my time with you." Eros said, moving so that he could kiss Peter. "You make me feel like I've never felt before. Everything feels so new with you."

The sensations coursing through his body had Eros feeling as if he had lightening running through his veins. Everything felt a thousand times better than it ever had, and he had thousands of years of experience, but nothing had ever felt like this.

"Oh, my mate, I should never have made you wait for me the way I did," Eros gently said, as he started to move his hand. "I'm so sorry. I never knew it would be this good."

"Eros!" Peter cried out. "Please...more."

Eros tightened the grip he had around their shafts, and he rubbed his thumb over their leaking heads.

"Close." Peter panted.

"You going to make me smell like you?" Eros could barely get the words out, but he was determined to drive Peter crazy and if one thing really hit a shifter's buttons, it was having a mate smell of them.

"Ugh."

He could feel how hard Peter was, knew he was about to come, and on the last drag of his hand to the top of their cocks, he let the tip on one of his fingernails dip into the small opening of Peter's dick.

"Eros!" Peter screamed.

The blast of wet warmth that began to coat their stomach's and pricks set off Eros's orgasm, and he added to the mess. The way that their cocks pulsed against one another kept sending electric jolts through Eros's system.

Feelings coursed through Eros, feeling he never thought he would ever feel. Love. Love for his mate. Now Eros understood why humans looked so hard for it. It left a person feeling exposed, and whole at the same time. Something settled in his soul, and Eros knew he'd finally found someone to call home.

Now that the edge is off... He thought with a grin.

Chapter Twelve

Peter was still shaking, his body rocking with the aftermath of the best orgasm of his life. His animal half had leaped forward when Eros grunted out his climax, determined to claim their mate. Holding him back was one of the hardest things Peter had ever done. But it was worth it, because as Eros held up a tube of lube, his eyes twinkling with lust, the warm pit in Peter's stomach grew and his cock, that never really went down, hardened again.

"I could wave my hand," Eros crooned in his ear, as his hand traveled down Peter's torso. "One wave of my hand and you'd be filled with lube, your hole stretched and ready for my cock. But as I said before, I want to take my time with you. We only get one claiming and I want yours to be truly special."

"It is special." Peter gulped as Eros's fingers tickled under his balls and went lower. "It's special because it's you."

"You say the sweetest things," Eros groaned and flexed his hip against Peter's thigh. Then he froze, and Peter looked up, sensing a change in mood immediately.

"What's wrong?"

"I'm being summoned. Damn it, that rarely ever happens." Eros sat up, his face scrunched almost as though he was in pain.

"You can be summoned?" Peter would have thought a god would be exempt from such things.

"It's very rare love comes with an or death clause, but fuck… I am so sorry, my darling Peter, but I have to go." Eros scrambled off the bed.

"Let me come too." Peter wondered where his clothes had been put. "Wave me up some pants. I might be able to help."

"Didn't you hear me? Love or death. It could be dangerous." Eros looked torn and Peter unashamedly took advantage of that.

"I want to see what you do. Please?"

Peter knew he'd won. He was suddenly clothed, including sturdy boots far better than anything he'd worn before.

"Hold onto my hand, and you don't interfere, no matter what," Eros warned. "They won't be able to see us, but even so, no matter what you see, stay quiet. Promise?"

Pressing his lips together, Peter nodded.

Letting out a long sigh, Eros clothed himself. "I'd far rather be claiming you than doing this," he muttered as they both disappeared from Peter's room.

***

Eros's heart sank as they arrived at the scene. They landed in a huge warehouse containing sixty plus cages. In other words, a slavery ring. Eros had lost count of how many of those he'd attended, curtailed by the Fates from saving every pitiful body locked up in a cage. He heard Peter's muffled gasp beside him and squeezed his hand, reminding him to be quiet. Not that any of the poor souls in the cages were in a state to notice anything out of the ordinary.

Eros's gift allowed him to pinpoint the poor wretch praying for him. To his shock, he realized his "client" was a shifter, but the tie between him and his mate was still silver. Claimed mate connections were always gold threads, getting thicker and stronger the longer the two individuals were together. The silver thread meant the two people had met, but hadn't claimed each other yet. The young man in question's thread was getting thinner and more frail by the minute. He was close to death.

Keeping a firm grasp of Peter's hand, Eros wafted them closer to the cage in question. The shifter was young, in his early twenties. His matted curls reminded Eros of Peter's, his slender face sporting a mass of bruises. Hunched over himself, the young man was babbling, and from what he was saying, he was resigned to his demise.

"Blessed Fates, don't let him see me like this, please, I beg you. I understand why he didn't want to be with me. I am unworthy, I know that. He'll feel responsible. He might die. Don't let that happen, please, in your mercy, don't let that happen. Let my Roderick find love again. Please."

His eyes filled with tears, Peter turned to him, the question evident in his eyes. Eros shook his head. The Fates could not be bargained with and if this young man died, then Roderick would spend at least the next hundred years alone. But all was not lost. Eros was only called to situations he could change. Following the silver thread, and taking care to hang onto his own mate, Eros drifted through the warehouse, passing through the walls, across a vacant parking lot, to a building on the other side of the street.

Police. A lot of them. Clearly the men were on their way to being rescued, but whether it was soon enough was another story. Ignoring the mass huddled around maps, arguing about entry points and other nonsense, Eros focused on a tall alpha, standing at the back of the room. From the clenched teeth, and the way the man kept flexing his fists, Roderick knew his mate was among the taken and wasn't happy with the rescue delay. Tapping into a little-used one of his gifts, Eros reached out mentally, searching for the man's thoughts.

All my fault... What if he's dead... My last memory of him... the hurt and anguish on his face. Fuck, I'm such a fool. So, what if he's young... so what if mom doesn't approve... fuck, who cares if the captain's human and doesn't know about mates, and doesn't approve of gays. All this standing around... he could be dying in there... why the hell can't they hurry up?

Do you want him? Eros prodded gently. Roderick froze, his eyes looking around.

Fates? Really? One of the Fates heard my call? Please, please save my mate.

Ignoring the Fates reference, but really couldn't he get some recognition once in a while, Eros whispered into Roderick's mind once more. *Duty or mate? Your man is close to death. Five minutes, and he'll be gone for good. You're an alpha wolf shifter. Do what you were born to do.*

Eros could see the man's hesitation – the way Roderick's eyes went from the men he clearly worked with and out the door where his mate lay dying. He couldn't prod the man any further and an arrow would be wasted on a shifter pair. The thread binding Roderick and his mate was now only the thickness of a hair. *Hurry! Please hurry.* Eros didn't realize he was clutching Peter's hand so tightly until his mate whispered in his ear.

"It's okay. Look, he's going now."

Sure enough, resolve etched over his handsome face, Roderick didn't give his boss a second glance as he strode from the room. A few of them called out to him, something about jeopardizing an operation, but Eros and Peter followed Roderick. Across the road, into the stinking warehouse, Roderick didn't falter until he got to the cage where his mate was still curled up, head bowed.

"You came." The young man couldn't seem to believe what he was seeing. "You have to get out of here. They'll be coming back soon. It's not safe for you here."

But even as the young man was talking, Roderick was pulling at the cage bars, bending them through the sheer force of his hands. As soon as the gap was big enough, Roderick pulled the young man free, tears in his eyes as he stroked gently over the man's bruises. "I've been such a stupid fool. I'll spend our whole lives together, putting your needs first, if you'll just say you forgive me."

"I've loved you from the moment I scented you at Denny's." As Eros watched them share their first kiss, the silver thread shimmered and thickened. Before sunrise, it would be gold. Eros would bet his arrows on it. Looking around, taking in the other cages, and the plight of the people in them, Eros threw out his hands, sending a wave of magic out to all four walls. Locks dinged, cage doors flew open. Young men in various states of health, staggered out, some helping others, some just falling to the ground.

"What the hell happened?" Roderick pulled back from his mate's lips long enough to ask.

"It's the power of Love, babe," the young man answered. "Kiss me again."

Eros and Peter disappeared.

Chapter Thirteen

"My gods, that was incredible," Peter yelled as they reappeared in his small apartment bedroom. "The way you pushed that guy into doing what was right. What did you say to him, anyway?"

Eros looked shocked. "You knew I talked to him in his mind?"

"I could feel it, sense it, I knew you did something." Peter was still buzzing from how powerful his mate was. "When those two kissed, I could feel the love." He hesitated, stroking down Eros's shoulder. "All those other people you set free from the cages. Will they be all right?"

Eros shrugged, and Peter could feel how uncomfortable he was. "It's not my place to say," Eros said haltingly. "You see there's the Fates, and free will…."

"I understand," Peter said quickly, nestling into his mate's side. "It must be so hard for you, seeing all the things you wish you could change, and that you have the power to change, but you can't because that's not how life works."

"You really do understand. I'm so lucky to have you by my side." Eros leaned on him, holding him close.

Peter's animal side, which was getting decidedly pushy for a claim, wanted to nuzzle and bite. The human side of Peter wanted a bed first, and Eros's cock deep inside of him.

"Did you need some time to get yourself together after helping those two men?" *Please say no, please say no.*

"And miss out on sinking into your delicious ass?" Eros shook his head. "Their thread won't be the only one gold in the morning."

Peter didn't have a clue what his mate was talking about, but when Eros tilted his head and they shared a kiss of their own, his blood got heated, all his thinking power went south, and Peter found he really didn't care what color the threads were. It was finally claiming time.

Pulling back from the kiss, Peter looked down at their clothed bodies.

"Naked, now."

Watching Eros wave his hand, they were both naked in a second. Peter reached over and grabbed his mate's hand, pulling him as he stepped back towards the bed.

"Need you, need to claim you," Peter growled, his shifter half was done waiting.

"Get on the bed, ass in the air," Eros ordered as he spun Peter around, so he was facing the bed.

Peter got on the bed and crawled until he was in the middle, making sure to put a little extra sway in his hips.

"Like this?" He asked, looking over his shoulder to see Eros staring at his ass.

"Oh, yeah," Eros whispered. "You are the most amazing man I have ever seen."

When Eros lifted his gaze and let it collide with Peter's, he was able to see the sincerity of his words in Eros's eyes.

"Make love to me," Peter said. "Bind us together for the rest of our lives, for as long as we live."

"I promise to be with you for as long as that is, my mate," Eros told him, as he got on the bed and moved so he was behind Peter.

Turning back around, Peter lowered his head and rested it on his arms.

He wasn't prepared to feel Eros running his tongue from his balls and over to the small of his back. Not sure who moaned louder, Eros or himself.

"You taste so good," Eros murmured, "I was going to take my time and taste you all over, but I can't wait."

"No, no more waiting," Peter demanded. His other half wanted them to be mated. They could take their time making slow love for the rest of their lives, but he needed Eros now.

The sudden feeling of his ass being stretched and ready left him gasping for air.

"I know I promised slow, but I can't wait," Eros moaned, "I need to feel you wrapped around my cock."

"Gods, yes," Peter yelled. "Please Eros, claim me."

Peter felt the bed move as Eros moved over him, pressing his front to Peter's back. Being able to feel his mate's heat surround him made Peter feel protected.

When he felt the blunt head of Eros's cock press up against his ass, Peter relaxed his muscles, eager to feel his body being filled by his mate.

"I'm going to love you so hard, forever."

Peter was able to hear the promise in those words.

"Yes…love…forever."

Peter was barely able to get the words out. The feeling of Eros slowly pushing into his body took all thoughts away, and Peter could only feel. Feel the hot, hard length of Eros as he breached the muscles of his ass, and slowly push all the way into him. He swore that he could feel Eros in the back of his throat. Holy hell, his mate was blessed, and so was he, since he got to spend the rest of his life enjoying it!

Once he was able to feel Eros's balls slapping against him, Peter just whined. He needed his mate to move.

"Hush mate, I will give you all you need and so much more," Eros whispered to him, then he began to slowly move.

Peter was ready to kill his mate, before they even finished their mating.

"Faster," He demanded. "Fuck me into this mattress, or I swear…" Peter wasn't able to finish that sentence, since Eros had shifted his body.

Holding Peter by the neck, he took his other hand and held him by the hip.

"Is this what you need my mate?"

Eros began to move faster, making sure that each stroke of his cock was moving over Peter's prostate. All

Peter could see were stars, as his body was no longer under his control.

"Are you going to come on my cock?" Eros growled out. "No touch to your cock, just me fucking you."

All Peter could do was whine again, the feeling of Eros and what he was doing to him was the only thing he could focus on. The way his ass was filled with that hard length and how it kept rubbing on his prostate.

"I'm going to make you come so hard, it will feel like your balls are going to come out the end of your dick." Eros kept talking to him, ramping up his desire and need to come.

"As soon as you start to come, your ass will clamp down tight on my cock. I'm going to fill you with my hot come, letting everyone know that you are mated. I'm going to mark you as my mate, and leave you dripping with my come."

Unable to take any more, Peter screamed out his release. Hot jets of come painted the bed under him. He was able to feel his ass tighten around Eros as his balls emptied their load.

Peter distantly heard Eros yell out his name as he felt the cock in his ass expand and pulse as he filled

Peter with his spunk. He could feel the warmth of it bathing his insides, when he suddenly felt a burning pain on his chest.

"EROS!" Peter yelled out for his mate, before the mix of bliss and pain caused him to pass out.

Chapter Fourteen

Eros quickly laid his mate down on the bed, making sure he first cleaned up the wet spot. He carefully rolled Peter over to see what was wrong.

He wasn't expecting to see the tattoo that was suddenly on Peter's chest, right over his heart.

"How…" Eros whispered, not even sure who he was asking.

"That is how others will know he is your mate." Atropos's voice was heard in the room. "When he wakes, you need to be prepared, as his other half will be more than ready to make you their mate."

Oh boy! Eros wondered, not sure if he was going to be dealing with Peter or his animal half. He hoped it was Peter, since he didn't think he would ever be ready for a cock like the one Peter would have in his shifted form. Sasquatch were big all over, ALL over and Eros hadn't been on the receiving end of things for a long while.

Hearing the low moan that Peter made, Eros quickly moved to lie beside him.

"Shh, mate." Eros rubbed Peter's stomach, hoping it offered some comfort. "I'm right here."

"Ouch. What happened?" Peter looked down to his chest. "What the hell!" Peter went to touch the area, but Eros put out his hand, blocking him.

"Careful," Eros admonished, "I don't know if it's still hurting you."

"No, I'm okay. I feel a bit of pain, but it's nothing severe. It's like a mild sunburn."

"I'm sorry, I didn't know this would happen." Eros said, kissing his mate's forehead. "I've never really dealt with any of the mates of the gods, but I would have warned you about this if I had known."

"I know you would have." Peter leaned up and kissed him. Soon the kisses turned heated and Eros knew his mate was gearing up for round two.

"Will you do me the honor of becoming my mate?" Peter whispered to him.

"Yes." As if there would ever be any other answer that he could or would give his gift from the Fates. He moved, lying on his back, so he could watch his mate's expressions.

"Have you ever done this before?" Eros softly asked.

"No," Peter turned a bright red with that admission, "but I've watched a lot of porn, and I love reading the gay romance books. They have some excellent information in them."

Eros had to laugh. Somehow, he didn't think the authors who wrote the books had "informing the public" in mind when they wrote their sex scenes. He also knew that he could take care of some of the prep, in case Peter's nerves got the better of him.

"Just remember, lube is our friend. You can never have too much of it."

Peter chuckled, losing the tension in his body, which was what Eros was going for.

"You know that I am going to fall so deeply in love with you, that you will forget what it was like to be alone." Peter leaned over Eros, looking into his eyes. "I make my vow to you now my mate, that I will be beside you for the rest of our lives, that you will never know a day again of not being loved by me."

Eros almost forgot to breathe, seeing the honesty of his words in Peter's gaze. He knew that he would have this man beside him for the rest of the lives. Peter was the perfect man to help and support Eros with his sworn duty, helping the world find love one match at a time.

"I look forward to spending the rest of eternity with you beside me." Eros lifted his arm to hold Peter's cheek in the palm of his hand. "I am so grateful that the fates matched us together."

Peter leaned down and kissed him, and it felt to Eros as if he was pouring all his love into the kiss. Soon, the gentle glide of their lips quickly became devouring.

"I need you mate." Peter growled out. "As much as I want to spend hours learning everything about your body, I need you."

It took Eros a few seconds to understand what Peter was saying, and he quickly got his body ready.

Moving so that his legs were wrapped around Peter's waist, leaving him open and waiting to feel Peter slide home in his body. Once he was able to feel the head of Peter's cock at his entrance, Eros made sure to add some extra lube.

Oh hell, he forgot the relaxing part.

Trying not to hold his breath, Eros was rewarded when he felt the head of Peter's cock move past the muscle and he could feel the pop. Feeling the slow movement of said cock taking its merry time filling him, Eros was ready to yell that he needed Peter. Now.

Just as he was about to say something, he groaned in pleasure when Peter rubbed against his prostate. He had forgotten how good it felt when someone rubbed against it.

"Yes, right there," Eros panted, "and don't stop. You miss that and I'll…"

"What will you do mate?" Peter asked, then he leaned down and began to suck on one of the pebbled nipples on his chest.

The only reply that Eros made was a low groan, not sure which way to move or how to speak. Peter was playing his body like a musical instrument. The way he could feel every vein in the hard cock that was sliding in and out of his ass, hitting and rubbing his prostate that had him ready to sing the Hallelujah Chorus. The way that Peter would bite his nipples and suck them to ease the pain. The hands roaming all over his body, making his skin sensitive to even the touch of air on it.

"Do you know that I'm going to bite you on the crook of your neck." Peter whispered to him. "I'm going to bite you and leave a nice large mating mark. Let everyone know that you are mated."

Eros could only drop his head back while Peter told him what he was going to do.

"Right here." Peter said, as he licked the area. "Leave a nice big mark"

"Peter...now." Eros was ready be beg.

He could feel his balls pulling up and his ass trying to keep the cock buried in him.

Hearing the roar coming from Peter as he sank his teeth into his neck should have frightened him, but all he could do was scream out his pleasure. His skin broke under the pressure, there was a brief moment of pain and then bliss filled every cell in his body. The silver thread showing their connection turned brilliant gold and thickened with every pulse of his heart. A fuzzy strength, a warm awareness filled the back part of his brain and Eros basked in it all, safe in the knowledge he was now completely bound to the only man who'd ever made the earth move for him. No one could ever break them apart.

Chapter Fifteen

It was dawn when Peter woke, hot sticky and with muscles aching where he didn't know he had muscles. Patting the area over his heart, the faint sting, almost non-existent now, reminded him the previous twelve hours hadn't been a dream. He was mated, claimed, bonded now to one person for the rest of existence. His snoring mate seemed more relaxed when he was sleeping, his giant mating scar glistening on his skin for all to see. Eros wasn't the only one sleeping, Peter's animal half was completely relaxed and oblivious to the world.

Dawn was Peter's favorite time of the day. The time when he'd be busy in the bakery kitchen, making doughs, kneading bread, creating delicious pastries that would provide a treat for everyone that popped into buy. Peter chewed his bottom lip. He couldn't hear anyone moving around downstairs. Cupid was probably on his way in, but Peter wanted to do something nice for his new friend. It hadn't been that long ago he and Harvey had been homeless. Now, they had a warm and safe place to stay, Peter was in his mate's arms, and he had a proper job. All of their good fortune came from Cupid interrupting his forage in the dumpster behind the café that day.

I could pop down for an hour, Peter reasoned with himself, watching his sleeping mate. *Get things prepped for when Cupid comes in and when he does, I can come up and make breakfast for Eros and Harvey. I'm sure Cupid won't mind, if I get a lot done before then.* Mind made up, Peter slipped out of bed, ducking into the adjoining bathroom. He could hear Harvey's snores rumble through the walls and mouthed a thank you to the Fates for keeping them both safe. A quick wash, Peter got dressed, checked he had the keys to the bakery and with a last long look at his mate, he left the room, crossing the living room and kitchen to release the fire escape door that served as the private entrance to the apartment.

Standing out on the small terrace area, Peter stretched, looking out over the rooftops to where the sun was tinting the sky in hues of pinks and yellows. It was going to be a glorious day and Peter's head was full of what he'd make for breakfast as he hurried down the wooden steps, ducking around the dumpster, pulling out his keys as he went. The lock was fiddly, almost loose, and Peter jiggled the key in the lock to make it turn. So intent on what he was doing, he didn't hear anyone approach until someone said, "Good morning, runt."

Turning, Peter's eyes widened. "You...." But anything else he might have said was lost. He felt a crashing blow to his skull and the world went black. His last thought was he wasn't going to make it for breakfast.

***

"Peter?" Eros woke with a start, to an empty bed and a cracking headache. "Peter?" He yelled more loudly. The door crashed open, but it wasn't Peter responsible, it was Harvey. The big man's hair was a mess, his chest was heaving, and his eyes were wild. Eros stared at the bright pink rabbits on his pajama bottoms, that hung low below a naked chest.

"Peter's been taken," Harvey said bluntly. "Hit on the head, taken."

"Surely not," Eros didn't think Peter would leave him sleeping the first day they were mated. Although the ache in his head was troubling. "Maybe he's in the bathroom and didn't hear us."

"I'm his twin, I know. You come." Harvey strode across the room, pulling Eros out of bed. Eros grabbed for his pants, but Harvey's grip and fast pace didn't allow him to put them on.

"Harvey, wait a second please." Eros wasn't going anywhere naked. "Let me get some pants on first."

"You're his mate. You should care." At least Harvey let go of his arm. Eros scrambled into his pants.

"I do care. We're mated now." Eros pointed to the scar on his shoulder. "I love Peter. It's our first day together. He wouldn't have left without telling me."

"What woke you up?" Leaning over, Harvey glared, his face inches from Eros's.

Eros touched the back of his head. "I'm not sure. One minute I was dreaming and the next I felt like someone hit me over the head."

"Not your head, Peter's." Harvey straightened up. "You have mate bond, I have twin bond, my animal told me Peter has been hurt. Now come. Quick."

Eros wondered, as Harvey led them through the small apartment, and down the stairs, why he was talking in shorthand. But as he watched a wave of hair appear and then disappear across Harvey's back, he understood. The poor shifter was hanging onto his animal form by a mere thread. The sense of urgency he was feeling seemed to get stronger and it wasn't all coming from Harvey. *Peter,* he whispered with his brain, but there was no response. Nothing but a black hole where Peter's energy had been the night before.

"He came past the dumpster." Harvey's shove moved the heavy thing at least six feet down the alley. Eros jumped out of the way. "He would have been opening the bakery. He does that. He likes to get things prepared before the day begins. I know my brother. He would have wanted to help Cupid to say thank you for the apartment."

"The door's still locked." Eros's eyes narrowed as he saw a set of shiny new keys dangling in the handle. "He didn't make it inside."

"Move your feet," Harvey grumbled, getting down on his hands and knees on the pavement.

Harvey was sniffing, just like a dog. *It's better than him doing that in shifter form,* Eros thought. Although it was still early, the last thing the shifters needed was a bigfoot sighting in down town Peakon. Lurching this way and that, Harvey was breathing hard when he got to his feet. "The bad man took Peter this way." He started to run down the block.

"Harvey, wait." But the big man didn't listen. Eros could zap to where Peter was, once the man was conscious, but it seemed the Fates had other ideas. Checking to make sure no one was watching, Eros waved himself some boots and shirt, before taking off after a distraught Harvey. *If something happens to his brother, Peter will never forgive me.*

Running to catch up to Harvey, he looked over and saw that he was still fighting to keep from shifting.

"Harvey, wait!" Eros yelled out, making sure he was ready to jump out of the way if Harvey got angry.

"I can find Peter when he's awake, I can zap to where he is once he opens the link between us." Eros said as he stepped up to stand in front of Harvey. "I give you my solemn promise that as soon as Peter wakes up, I will be beside him and take care of whoever dared to hurt my mate. I may be the god of love, but that doesn't mean that I won't end this person. I will destroy them in seconds."

Linking his arm with Harvey's, Eros turned them so that they were heading back to the apartment. Eros kept up a conversation with him, because he didn't want anyone to hear the growling noises coming from Harvey.

"I know you're angry, and you have a right to be." Eros snarled out the words, "but this person took my mate. I will leave them in the pits of Tartarus for the rest of eternity. No one touches Peter."

Eros didn't even realize that he was getting as angry as Harvey.

"Shhh, pretty man." Harvey said, patting him on the head, seeming a lot calmer. "Can't get so mad outside, peoples can't see you. Gotta hide the special, mom told me that."

Eros smiled at Harvey, "Yes, you are special. A very special man Harvey. When the time comes and you meet your mate, I will be with Peter while we celebrate such a special time for you."

"I have mate?" Harvey started to look around, "Where?"

"Not yet, Harvey, but you will be meeting with him soon."

"Thank you, pretty man." Harvey patted him on the head again. "I'm getting a man, I was scared it would be a girl." The whispered horror in that last word almost had Eros laughing, but he could see how serious Harvey was.

"Come on, big guy. Let's go back to the apartment and try to wait patiently for Peter to wake up. I'll go to him as soon as he does."

"Fine." Harvey said, then stomped off towards the apartment.

"What the hell happened here?" Cupid yelled from the alley, where the dumpster had been.

"Bad man took Peter." As soon as he finished saying that, Harvey broke out bawling. "I want my brother."

Chapter Sixteen

The first thing that Peter felt was pain. His head hurt so badly, he was dizzy and trying not to throw up.

Attempting to lift his hand, he found that they were tied tightly behind his back, and his legs were tied together too. If he tried to shift, he would ruin his shoulders. He rolled over and threw up all over the floor he was lying on.

"Really, did you have to do that," A man's voice said. "Oh, that stinks."

"What did you expect, you hit me pretty hard. I think you gave me a concussion," Peter choked out, spitting out what was left in his mouth. He wasn't going to agree with whoever had him, but it was pretty gross.

"Why did you do this?" Peter finally looked over to the guy. He recognized the leader of the gang who'd tried to hurt him outside the homeless shelter. "I've never done anything to you. Why are you doing this?"

"You took my father away from me!" The guy screamed at him.

Peter winced at the sound of his voice. Didn't the guy know how to use his indoor voice?

"Father, as in my father?" Peter wondered what he was talking about. He and Harvey were still kids when their father died, and his mom had never gotten over it. Peter used to think she'd have faded away to nothing if she hadn't been so intent on raising them properly.

"We have the same father." The guy got up and stomped around in agitation. "He left me and my mom when he met your mom. Apparently, your mom was his mate."

"I don't understand. If Mom knew about you, she would never have kept our dad away from you." Peter told him. "She would have welcomed you into our home as one of her own."

"Ha. That's what you think. Dear old dad wanted nothing to do with me when he found out I couldn't shift. I was some kind of throwback or something. The shifter gene completely skipped me, and how unfair was that? Both my parents were shifters. My mom almost killed me when she found out I couldn't shift. She told me dad didn't want me anymore."

"No disrespect intended but I think your mom was spinning you a line. Dad never mentioned having another family and my mom would've welcomed you with open arms." Peter didn't think the guy was even listening to him.

"Then how do you explain why I was adopted out. My mom took me after dad left and gave me to another couple saying Dad could never bear to look at my face again. They were happy enough to keep me around. Adopting a kid was far cheaper than paying a hired hand to work on the farm. Do you know what it's like to get whipped to get out of bed? The first time they whipped me I was fifteen. Do you have any idea how much that hurt? I swear they enjoyed hearing me screaming and begging them to stop."

Peter almost threw up again, thinking of the horrors his half-brother had lived through.

"But I got even with them." The guy stopped and stared at Peter with dead eyes. The shiver that ran down his spine at seeing the vacant look in them was frightening.

"I waited. I bided my time and then one night, when they'd had too much to drink, I trapped them in their bed. I tied them up, one arm each to the bed post and the other arms joined together so they could not move. They were awake then and they knew that death was coming. I can still remember the stench of the gas I used to pour all over them and the bed, and the screaming that started when I lit the match. But just like them, when I was screaming, I didn't even look at them as I walked away." The man inhaled, as if he could still smell the gasoline, a twisted smile on his face. "The whole damn house burned to the ground and I did nothing to stop it."

Peter shuddered, the visions of the screams and the flames vivid in his head.

"Do you know what else I did?" The guy asked him, as if they were having a conversation over a cup of coffee.

"No," Peter whispered.

"I found dad. Oh, it was completely random although I had been looking for him. I knew what town he was staying in, but I didn't have an address. Imagine my surprise when I saw him one day, playing with you guys in a park. You were only little kids, but you were all laughing and having a great time."

The man's agitation was increasing. Peter flinched as some of his kicks got too damn close for comfort.

"What did you do?" Maybe if he could keep the man talking, help would arrive. Yeah, he was always an optimist, go him.

"I followed you all home. He didn't even notice me. I waited until Dad was leaving for work one day. He was so shocked, but then happy to see me. He wanted to bring me into the house to meet his mate and kids," the man snorted. "As if I wanted to meet that bitch or you brats."

"But don't you see?" Peter said desperately. "Your mom must have been wrong about him all along. Maybe she told him you'd run away from home or something. Maybe she told him you refused to see him."

"My mom didn't have any reason to lie to me," the man snarled. "He left her, and then he got his."

"What happened?" Peter already knew his father was dead. But to think....

"I was cool about everything. I told him I wasn't ready to meet you yet and asked if he wanted to go out and get some breakfast."

The maniacal laughter falling from that twisted mouth had all the hairs on Peter's body standing on end.

"I asked him if he would like to maybe go somewhere quiet where we could talk without any interruptions, so we went to the same park I had seen him playing with you and that brother of yours. He drove us, spouting all this shit about how the fates must have intervened and how we could all be a family again. Bullshit. Just as he put the car into park, I shot him in the head. Even a shifter can't recover from that."

The glint in his eyes told Peter the man had enjoyed killing their father. He'd also ensured that the injuries suffered were permanent, because shifters could heal from most things.

"After I was sure he was dead, I put him in the back of the car and drove it to a lake and let the car drive into it. He was gone, just like those bastards who beat me."

Peter thought the story was finished. The man's eyes were like looking into evil personified. Peter struggled to believe someone so depraved could be related to him and sweet Harvey. Harvey, who'd probably noticed he was gone and was probably having a fit. Him and Eros both. *Fates, keep them safe,* Peter thought as the man took up his story again.

"Someone had seen what I had done, and they asked me if I wanted to work for them. Turns out, he was someone who worked as an assassin. I thought 'why not'. I figured I could earn some good money doing the jobs, while getting some good training from him."

"Is that why you waited to come after us? Because you were busy learning how to kill people?"

"Nope, I waited until I knew if you could shift or not. I would have let you guys live if you didn't shift, but since you did, you had to be put down."

"But why kill my mom? She wasn't a shifter," Peter asked, tears in his eyes as remembered his mother's brutalized body and all the blood on the floor.

"Because if dad hadn't of met that bitch, I would have had a family. I would have been happy," he snarled, kicking Peter squarely in the ribs.

Peter screamed when he felt something snap in his chest.

Peter! He heard Eros scream his name in his mind.

Eros, help, was the last thought Peter had before the blackness claimed him again.

Chapter Seventeen

Legend and folklore depicted Eros/Cupid as a cute little kid in a diaper, or at best, as a scantily clad adolescent with a sweet little bow and arrow. The Eros that landed in the room Peter was being held in was nothing like that. Fury rolling off him like a wave, Eros swept his hand in front of him, sending the man kicking the hell out of his mate smashing into the concrete wall.

"Who are you to hurt my mate?" Eros roared. "Who gave you the right to touch the mate of a god?"

"Bullshit. You ain't a god." But Eros could see the man licking his lips, looking between where he was standing and the door. "The door was locked. How the hell did you get in here?"

"Hell had nothing to do with my being here," Eros snarled, looking deep inside the man's soul and hating what he could see. There were no connections, no threads tying the man to anyone. Instead his life thread was completely entangled around his black and bitter heart. "But believe me, I can call Hades for you if you want. I'm sure Hades would be happy to see you strung up and tortured for eternity by his many demons if I ask him nicely. I hear the demon king Balthazar got sick of his latest plaything recently, when the man's voice box gave out. No point in torturing a person if you can't hear them screaming is it?"

The man gulped. "Hey man, I don't know who the hell you are, or how you got in here, but what I do with my brother is family business. It has nothing to do with you."

Brother? I thought Harvey… Yeah, the family discussion could wait for later. Eros's eyes narrowed as he saw the man sneak a gun into his hand. "Oh no," he said in mock horror, throwing up his hands, "are you going to shoot me?"

"I'll teach you to interfere in my business."

The gun rang out. Eros dissipated just enough so the bullet would pass through him and then materialized again. "Oops, you missed. Did you want to try that again?"

"What the fuck," the man looked down the barrel of his gun. "I never miss."

Eros clicked his finger and thumb together. The gun rang out a second time and the intruder was now splat on the floor with a bullet where his third eye should be. "You didn't miss that time. Have fun in hell asshole."

A harsh groan pulled him from his perusal of the body. "Eros?" Peter's voice was weak and his breath wheezy. "What happened? Did you kill him?"

"No," said Eros stepping over the body, so he could reach his mate. The ropes binding Peter disappeared with a wave of his hand, but Peter was still looking at him, his eyes sad and full of pain. Eros risked a glance at the ceiling. "He shot himself. An accident with his gun, I imagine." *It was close enough,* he sent to the Fates. *He was holding the gun when it went off.* A light chuckle in his head Eros let know he wasn't in any trouble. "Are you all right." Peter's safety was his only concern. "Me and Harvey have been really worried about you."

"He said he was my brother. That we had the same father. He was born before Dad even met my mother." Peter's eyes were full of tears. "He killed everyone. His foster parents, my mom and dad. He's been after us all this time… Eros why?"

"Oh baby," Eros pulled Peter into his arms as carefully as he could. "Some people just have a black heart and don't see the world the way you do."

"But I would've loved him." Peter was sobbing openly now. "My mom, my dad, they would have all given him the family he was looking for, if he'd just given them a chance. He didn't have to kill them."

Eros sighed heavily, near to tears himself, although he'd never admit it. "Babe," he said, struggling to know what to say to make his mate feel better. "Sometimes, despite the best efforts of the fates, and the gods, and every other higher power there is, some people choose to behave in a cruel or nasty way. That is what free will is all about. Humans, shifters, even gods, we're not playthings of some higher deity, we can all choose how to respond to the different situations we come across in life. You choose a higher path when your mom was killed. You took Harvey, looked after him and did all you could to be the best you could be. Now you can do that without having a psychotic killer on your tail. You and Harvey are safe now, don't you see?"

Swallowing hard, Peter nodded. "Do you, would you mind if I shifted for a quick minute? I'm fairly sure my ribs are broken, and I know I'm covered in bruises. I can't scent anyone else around so it would be safe. I don't want Harvey to see me like this. It was bad enough you had to."

"I'll admit, this battered and bruised look you're rocking at the moment, is not your best look," Eros said with a smile to show he was teasing. "I've been wanting to see your shifted form since you mentioned what he was. But don't take too long. Harvey is going nuts without you."

"I'll be quick, I promise." Peter reached up, pecking Eros lightly on the cheek, before wincing. "Can you help me with my shirt? And don't be surprised if my sasquatch gets cuddly. He really wants to meet you and for you to admire his fur."

Eros agreed, which was why, five minutes later he was sitting on a giant Sasquatches' knee, brushing the beast's fur and telling him how strong and handsome he looked. Which was true.

Chapter Eighteen

"Peter!" The loud cry was the only warning he had before he and Eros were grabbed into a huge hug from Harvey. Moments later, he was gasping for air, but Harvey had thankfully put him down.

"You okay?" Harvey was turning him around, checking to make sure he was all right.

"I'm fine Harvey." Peter held his hand out to Eros. "My mate got rid of the bad guy and let me shift to heal my headache."

Please don't tell him everything, I don't want Harvey to be upset Peter sent to his mate. He knew that Eros understood when he simply nodded.

Harvey swung his head to look at Eros. "You mean it, pretty man? No more bad guy? He's gone?"

"I promise you Harvey, he is gone. He is now residing in a special place with Hades, never to bother you again."

Peter had to laugh at the look on Eros's face when Harvey grabbed him into a huge hug. "Thank you for getting Peter," Harvey said, while trying to squeeze all the air out of his lungs.

"Glad I could help, big guy," Eros gasped.

"What the hell happened?" A very angry Cupid ranted, as he stomped over to where Harvey had gone back to checking Peter again. "I come in to work to find Harvey in tears and worried about Peter, only to be told that you suddenly disappeared with no word. Do you have any idea how hard it was trying to understand what Harvey was saying when he's that distraught? He was so scared, and he was having problems telling me what was wrong."

Cupid came over and starting to fuss over Harvey. "Come with me, I'll get you a nice warm drink and something to eat."

"Hey, what about us?" Eros asked.

"Hmpf. You both seem fine to me." After saying that, Cupid started to gently move Harvey towards the shop, still clucking at him.

Peter could only smile at the scene they made. He was so grateful that he was found by Cupid trying to find something to eat in his dumpster. Now, he had a mate and found a home.

"So, someone want to explain to me what the fuck happened?" A growling Liam asked as he came up the alley behind them. "You left Harvey in tears and then you upset my husband. No one gets to upset Cupid like that."

"Come upstairs and we'll explain," Peter said, grabbing Eros's hand. "I don't want to speak about it out in the open."

Peter led the way, and as soon as he got into the apartment, he went to the kitchen to make some coffee.

"Eros, can you start explaining while I get changed into some fresh clothes?"

"Sure." Eros went over to the couch and sat down. "Have a seat, this might take a while."

As Eros started with how he woke with a headache, he proceeded to tell him his side of the story, and how he had managed to calm Harvey down with the promise that as soon as Peter would wake up, he would be able to go to where he was. The unfortunate part of that was the Eros had to wait until Peter woke, as that was how the mating worked. Peter sat down just as Eros was getting to the part about calming Harvey down.

"Wait, you're saying that you can speak to each other in your minds?" Liam looked shocked, then intrigued. "Could something like that be done for Cupid and I?"

"I can do that for you, but let's wait and get his permission as well. Somehow I don't think he would be happy with either of us if I just did it."

The look of fear on Liam's face was comical, and Peter had a hard time not laughing.

"Uhh…let's wait and ask him." The tender smile on Liam's face reinforced the fact to Peter that Cupid was well loved by this man. "He can get pretty feisty when he's pissed."

Peter looked at Eros in surprise when he barked out a quick laugh. *Tell you later* Eros whispered to him.

"So, it turned out that this man was my half-brother." Peter began to tell his side of events. "He hit me over the head as I was about to go to the shop and start the daily setup to make it easier for Cupid. When I woke up, he started to rant about what had happened and how his mother abandoned him when it was discovered that he couldn't shift. By the time that happened, our father had already left them since my mom was his mate. He killed his adoptive parents due to the physical abuse they were putting him through."

"It was sometime after that he was approached by someone who was an assassin of some type, who taught him everything else anyone needed to know about killing people." Peter felt the tears forming in his eyes. "He eventually found us. He saw our father playing with us at a nearby park. He approached him one morning as he was leaving for work, took him to that park and murdered him. The only reason mom was able to survive the loss of her mate was because of us. He came back and killed her after we'd shifted, in an effort to get to us too."

Eros grabbed him and pulled him into his arms, while all Peter could do was cry over the loss of his parents.

"I was listening to him rant about what he felt were personal slights against him," Eros took over the story. "I can understand about the anger towards adoptive parents, because how he was treated was horribly wrong, but he had no reason to go after Peter and his family. They were innocents in all of this. The problem was by then the mental damage had been done, he was beyond saving. Killing tears an irreparable part of a person's soul. When I looked into his heart and saw the blackness, I knew he was too far gone to ever be redeemed."

"So, what happened to him?" Liam asked. "Where is he now?"

Peter could feel the kiss that Eros placed on the top of his head.

"He's now a permanent resident with Hades in the Underworld. What will happen to him for the rest of eternity will be up to him. Hades can be inventive with some of the punishments he gives out. But here, on this realm no one will ever have to worry about him again."

"Does anyone know what happened to the man's mother? The one who sold him?" Peter could understand this was Liam's detective mode coming into play. It was who he was.

"He never mentioned seeing her again." Peter thought about how protective his half-brother had been of her, even after she'd sold him. "It's highly possible, if he did seek her out at any time, any negativity he got from her he'd have wiped from his mind. In his delusions, he saw nothing wrong with his mother getting rid of him and when I questioned what she'd said about our father, he defended her."

"Unfortunately, that's the nature of a delusional mind," Liam agreed. "I've seen countless cases of children being abused by their parents, and yet still insisting they are loved and wanting to go back with them. I'll run a check through our system, more to make sure she never had any more offspring than anything else. She shouldn't be too hard to trace through our computers if she was married to your father, before he mated with your mother."

Peter shivered at the thought of a mean person out there, still making hell in the lives of young ones.

"Is there going to be a problem, with me disposing of the killer like I did?" Eros asked. His tone was casual, but Peter could sense he was worried. "You should know, as a man of the law, that because I'm a god, I can never be put in jail, or go through your justice system. You wouldn't even be able to register my fingerprints. And I'll tell you now, in all honesty, death was too good for that man. You didn't see what I saw in his heart."

Liam sat back for a moment and thought about it. "As a detective, I could never condone someone taking the law into their own hands, even if it's fully justified like it is in this case. But no case has actually been filed. It's not as though I have to go back to my Captain and explain to him how a killer ended up dead, and why I don't see the need to investigate it. The Hades option was probably the best outcome for everyone concerned. If we arrested him, there would be the chance he could get away and come back to further hurt someone. At least this way I don't have to worry about him hanging around my friends and family anymore."

While Eros and Liam continued to talk, Peter snuggled into his mate, happy to be home, safe and sound. He was looking forward to being able to help Eros with his task of helping others find the love of their lives, but he was also glad he could still keep working with Cupid. He loved being able to create something that brought joy to others. That was his last thought before he fell asleep, wrapped safely in his mates loving embrace.

Epilogue

Harvey was so happy. Peter had managed to find them a home, and Liam helped him to get a job.

Harvey knew he had some problems with his mind, but that didn't mean he was stupid. It just took him a bit longer to understand some things, but he always worked things out eventually.

"Peter, I'm going to work now." Harvey called out from the back door of the coffee shop that he worked in.

"Did you grab the lunch I left for you?" Peter called out. "Would you like a coffee to go and a warm apple turnover?"

"Warm?" Harvey asked, as his tummy rumbled at the thought of eating one of his favorite snacks. "Please?"

It was part of their morning ritual, and it helped to calm Harvey, knowing that everything in his life was safe.

He grabbed the thermos of coffee that Peter gave him and put it in his backpack, but kept the bag of the turnovers in his hand. He didn't want them to get accidently broken in the bag. Besides, how could he eat them if they were in there.

Giving his brother a hug, Harvey turned to walk to work.

"Have a great day." Peter called out, and Harvey gave him a smile and a wave as he turned the corner onto the sidewalk.

As he walked towards the job site where the construction crew was building a bunch of new homes, he was wondering what smelled so yummy.

Looking around, he wasn't able to see where is was coming from, but it seemed strongest over by the small forested area near the park.

Forgetting all about going to work, Harvey continued to follow the delicious scent. The only problem is he couldn't understand why it seemed to come from a small bush.

Getting down on his knees, he was surprised to see a small nose twitching at him. Seeing the cute little bunny, Harvey slowly put his hand out.

"Hi, are you okay little bunny?"

Harvey was worried at how small the bunny was. The bunny smelled scared and he could be hurt. Harvey knew his big size made him seem intimidating to most people, and he struggled to think of how he could let the little critter know he was one of the good guys.

"Would you like some of my apple turnover?" He offered, holding out the bag. "My brother makes them at a nearby bakery and they are the best thing ever. I'll share them with you if you like."

Harvey watched, barely able to breathe as the little bunny slowly limped out of the bushes, climbing up into his lap. His back leg seemed to be a funny angle, but Harvey couldn't smell the nasty scent of blood. Wondering if rabbits even ate apple turnovers, he fished around in the bag and broke off a small piece, holding it in the palm of his hand.

There was a shimmer, Harvey remembered happening when he shifted, and all of a sudden, instead of a bunny, there was a naked man on his lap.

"Oh, wow, shifter bunny." Harvey's face cracked open in delight.

"I am indeed," the little bunny man said, plucking the piece of apple turnover from Harvey's palm. "Hello, mate."

About the Authors

Dani Gray:

I've been an avid reader for as long as I can remember. I still remember one of the first books I read, it was the *Bobbsey Twins*. As I got older, I moved into more the interesting books, but some of the typo's made me nuts! So, after contacting writers I started a career of where I began content editing, beta reading and brainstorming. After being harassed for a couple of years by some of the writers, I gave in and have now begun to write.

I live in central Canada with my hubby of over 25 years, 4 kids, and 5 grandkids. We have a collection of pets, including our guard cat. I love nothing more than curling up with a good book, or my laptop to work on the next thing that catches the muse, much to the frustration of my hubby. I would love to hear from readers, you can find me at any of these places below. I promise, I'm bad at updating my blog, but I never ignore a question sent to me.

Blog: https://authordanigray.blogspot.com/

Facebook:

https://www.facebook.com/author.dani.gray

MeWe:

https://mewe.com/group/5b256bafa5f4e50e605dbac2

Email me at authordanigray@gmail.com

Lisa Oliver:

Lisa Oliver had been writing non-fiction books for years when visions of half dressed, buff men started invading her dreams. Unable to resist the lure of her stories, Lisa decided to switch to fiction books, and now stories about her men clamor to get out from under her fingertips. With over fifty MM true mate titles to her credit so far, Lisa shows no sign of slowing down.

When Lisa is not writing, she is usually reading with a cup of tea always at hand. Her grown children and grandchildren sometimes try and pry her away from the computer and have found that the best way to do it is to promise her chocolate. Lisa will do anything for chocolate.

Lisa loves to hear from her readers and other writers (I really do, lol). You can catch up with her on any of the social media links below.

Facebook –

http://www.facebook.com/lisaoliverauthor

Official Author page –

https://www.facebook.com/LisaOliverManloveAuthor/

My new private teaser group - https://www.facebook.com/groups/540361549650663/

My blog - (http://www.supernaturalsmut.com)

Twitter – http://www.twitter.com/wisecrone333

Email me directly at yoursintuitively@gmail.com.

Manufactured by Amazon.ca
Bolton, ON

14734931R00092